Discontent

E. H. Reinhard

AUTHOR'S NOTE

This book is a work of fiction by E. H. Reinhard. Names, characters, and incidents are products of the author's imagination or are used fictitiously. Any resemblance to actual events or persons, living or dead, is entirely coincidental. Locations used vary from real streets, locations, and public buildings to fictitious residences and businesses.

The scanning, uploading, and distribution of this book via the Internet or any other means without the permission of the publisher is illegal and punishable by law. Please purchase only authorized electronic editions and do not participate in or encourage electronic piracy of copyrighted materials. Your support of the author's rights is appreciated.

For more books by E.H. Reinhard, please visit:
http://ehreinhard.com/

CHAPTER 1

Manny

Manny cut the engine on the twenty-four-foot Yellowfin bay boat and coasted to the dock. Some of the homes around the canal were still lit inside. The time inched up on one in the morning.

"Get those buffs over your face," Manny said. He pulled his up from around his neck. "Glove up."

Paul and Eric, the two towering men accompanying Manny, did as instructed.

The dock they drifted toward belonged to a big vacant home. Manny had been there earlier in the week and had a look around.

"Gentlemen," Manny called out.

A pair of men waited on the unlit dock. The cherry from one of their cigarettes glowed in the night air.

"We've been out here waiting for a half hour," one of the men said.

The boat touched the dock, and Paul tied it up.

Manny stepped onto the dock and walked to the men.

He took each of them in—one of the guys was tall and thin, the other short and wide. "We're going to take a ride," Manny said through the buff wrapped around his face. Everything from his nose down was covered, and he wore an all-black hat over his shoulder-length dreadlocks.

"Where's Tavaras?" the shorter of the two men asked.

Manny had met the guys once before. Both were dressed in suits. The taller, long-haired one was going by the name Ken Winter, and the shorter, bald one had said his name was Aaron Kraft. Neither name was real.

"Tavaras doesn't know about this meeting. He's simply a middleman."

"Where are we going?" Kraft asked.

"You'll see when you get there," Manny said.

"What about our cars?" Winter asked.

"They'll be fine. This is one of our boss's properties."

"Your boss?" Winter asked. "Who the hell is your boss? We need to talk to Tavaras."

"You wanted to meet the Krokodil man, and now the Krokodil man wants to meet you."

"I need to make a call," Kraft said.

"No," Manny said. "But it's good that you mentioned you had a phone." Manny let out a quick whistle, and Eric and Paul stepped up on the dock from the boat. "Search these two. Everything in the water."

"What the hell," Winter said.

"Boss's orders. It is what it is. You'll be reimbursed," Manny said. He crossed his arms over his chest and watched as wallets and phones were pitched into the bay. The weapons went next—two guns off Winter, a single pistol from Kraft. Paul removed a small device and ran it up and down both men—legs, arms, torso, and back.

"What the hell is this?" Winter asked.

"Checking you for a transponder," Manny said.

"Why the hell would I have a transponder?" Winter bristled.

"They're clean," Paul said.

"Good. Let's go. In the boat," Manny said.

Eric and Paul led Winter and Kraft into the boat. Manny waited until the men were in before he stepped off the dock. Eric pulled the ropes. Manny fired the Yellowfin's single three-hundred-horsepower engine and made his way back out onto Biscayne Bay. As soon as he could open it up, he did. The boat normally did sixty miles an hour easy across calm water. With Manny's two hundred and fifty pounds, plus Eric and Paul, who were around three hundred pounds each, the boat's speedometer never rose above forty.

Manny pointed the boat toward Key Biscayne, a small island town south of Miami Beach. With a single causeway connecting the small strip of island to the mainland, the northernmost portion of the island being a county park and the southernmost a state park, privacy was all but guaranteed. The homes on the island fetched hefty sums. Inland, the homes averaged a couple million, and on the water, they averaged twenty. But the home that Manny was headed for was somewhere north of thirty, or so he figured. At the end of a peninsula, facing the Bill Baggs state park, was an eight-thousand-square-foot home nestled into the thick landscaping of the almost two-acre compound. From the water, all that could be seen of the buildings were a few rooflines among the palm trees. Beside the dock that wrapped the seawall was a manmade beach and a few cabanas. It wasn't until they passed the wall of trees lining the perimeter that they could see the grandeur of the grounds themselves. The ride across the bay took the better part of twenty minutes. Key Biscayne approached, growing larger and larger with each passing minute.

Manny slowed and pointed the boat toward the channel in between Baggs park and the properties on his left. The park off to his starboard side was pitch-black. To their port side, a few homes lit the darkness from behind their lush landscaping, pools, and manicured yards. Straight ahead came the light from the flames of a handful of tiki torches, and Manny slowed the boat to a crawl. The lights from his boss's expansive estate were visible through the gaps in the trees.

"Beach it," a man called out.

To Manny's ears, the voice sounded like Justin's, but all he saw was a shadow of someone on shore.

Manny drove the bow of the boat into the white sand beach and confirmed that the voice telling them to beach it was Justin's. Justin wore a tank top and board shorts. Tattoos covered his thin frame from feet to throat. Eric tossed a line off the front, and Justin staked it out.

"He's waiting," Justin said. "Up at the bar."

Winter and Kraft stepped from the front of the boat with Eric and Paul following. Manny hopped down and fist-bumped Justin as he walked past and followed the guys up the path. Through the line of palm trees and thick landscaping that provided privacy from the water, the grounds opened to a big illuminated pool. Manny looked past the pool at the thirty-foot-wide pergola, covered in vines and standing over a long wooden beach-themed bar. Lights dangled from the pergola's slats. Behind the bar was a pair of shelves stocked with bottle upon bottle of booze. Above the liquor was a big television. Matt, who was Manny's boss, and his brother Frank sat at the bar with two women. Manny couldn't remember the females' names off the top of his head. Behind the bar, another blonde in a bikini poured shots. Manny recognized her as Tiffany, or so she'd said earlier in the evening. From the back, Matt and Frank were hard to distinguish. Both were wide-shouldered and had tightly shaved gray-and-black hair. Matt and Frank both wore casual clothing, as if they'd been lounging around the pool all day, which was exactly what they had been doing and precisely what Manny had been doing until he went to pick up Winter and Kraft.

Manny followed the group around the pool, toward the bar, and immediately noticed that Matt was wearing two pistols in a dual gun shoulder holster. Matt hadn't been wearing guns before Manny left.

"Here comes the best part," Frank said. He pointed at the television.

One of the men on television came up and drove an ice pick into the side of the other's head.

Frank laughed, and one of the women winced. The fact

that Frank found enjoyment in the scene was fitting—he was as lethal and depraved as they came.

Matt, tan and in his late forties, nodded his approval of the murder while he finished the drink in his hand. He turned around and noticed the approaching group. Matt set his empty glass on the bar. "Ah, you guys finally made it," he said. "I thought I heard a boat." Matt clicked off the television and turned on his chair. "Frank, why don't you take the ladies inside for a bit?"

"You sure?" Frank asked.

"Yeah, go ahead," Matt said.

Frank slid off his stool. "Ladies, you heard the man. Get inside," he said. The women each did a shot of booze and started up the path to the house. Frank gave the last woman a playful slap on the butt to speed her up. She jumped and yelped.

Matt crossed his arms over his floral button-down shirt and scratched at his short black-and-gray beard as he watched Frank and the women disappear into the back of the house.

Eric and Paul led Winter and Kraft to within a few feet of Matt.

"You're good there," Matt said. His words, and Paul's outstretched arm, stopped Winter and Kraft from getting any closer to the boss. Eric and Paul stood to the sides of the guests. From a good five feet away, Winter reached out for a handshake. Matt declined with a wave of his hand. He stared at the two men, who returned his gaze.

Manny left Paul, Eric, Winter, and Kraft and walked behind the bar to pour himself a drink. He grabbed a bottle of gin and filled a rocks glass with ice.

"So, you're the real estate guys?" Matt asked.

Winter paused for a moment while he looked around. Kraft said nothing.

"I asked if you were the real estate guys," Matt repeated. "The ones who seem to be doing whatever they can to let people know that they're in the transportation business and available for hire."

Manny poured himself a drink and watched the situation begin to unfold.

"We put the word out that we were looking for new business, yes. Who are you?" Winter asked.

"I'm the man," Matt said.

"Where is Tavaras?" Kraft asked.

Matt turned his back on Winter and Kraft and looked at Manny behind the bar. "They've been searched?"

"Yeah," Manny said. "No weapons. No phones. No bugs or wires." He took a drink of his gin and looked over at Winter and Kraft. He could see concern on both their faces.

"Vests?" Matt asked.

Manny shook his head.

"Good. Fill me up. The Macallan. Neat." He slid his empty glass toward Manny.

"Yeah, no sweat," Manny said. He reached for one of the bottles.

"No. Not the twenty-one. Grab the one that says twenty-five on it," Matt said.

"Sure." Manny grabbed the bottle Matt wanted and splashed two fingers' worth into the glass. He slid it back to Matt.

Matt took a drink then examined the liquid in his glass for a moment before setting it down. He spun on his stool and faced the men. "Why don't you two come with me," Matt said. "We're going to go down to that shed over there and have a little talk."

"What?" Kraft asked.

"I'm fine with talking here," Winter said.

"We're going to go down to that shed," Matt repeated. "Let's go." He rose from his seat and waved for the men to follow.

Manny walked from behind the bar. Eric and Paul started toward the shed. Matt stopped. "Just me and these two," he said. He gave Manny a grab on top of the shoulder. "I'll be just fine."

"Um, okay. If you're sure," Manny said.

Matt nodded then pointed Kraft and Winter toward the white shed with the tile roof near the water. Manny watched as they entered, and Matt closed the door behind them.

"What the hell was that all about?" Eric asked.

"I don't know," Manny said. He went behind the bar to his drink. Minutes passed. Eric and Paul had joined Manny at the bar, and each popped a beer. Manny's mind was deep in thought. What could possibly be going on inside the shed, he didn't know. Why he wasn't asked to be in the shed, he didn't know. What he did know was that the two men were undercover cops—knowledge that Matt shared.

Manny lifted his gin. His eyes were locked on the windows of the shed that faced the pool area. Muzzle flashes lit the windows, accompanied by the sound of gunshots.

Manny paused with his glass a few inches from his lips. Eric and Paul turned on their stools and faced the shed. No one moved. The door on the shed opened, and Matt walked out.

Manny took a drink from his glass and set it down.

CHAPTER 2

A stop sign affixed to an arm swung out from the guard shack and blocked our entrance into the neighborhood. A white-haired man looking somewhere in his seventies emerged from the building before I got the car stopped. I lowered my window as he walked to the side of our cruiser.

"Morning," he said. He crouched and looked in my window. "Here with everyone else?"

I guessed he was referring to whoever was already on the scene that we'd been called to.

"I imagine so," I said. "We're looking for Ocean Mist Court."

"That's a yes, then. I'll get the gate for you. You'll go straight until this road ends, make a left, and Ocean Mist will be three blocks down on your right."

"Appreciate it," I said.

The guard gave me a nod and went back into the building, and the gate rose. Steve and I passed through, and I made a left at the end of the subdivision's entrance road.

"Check this out," Steve said.

He held his phone out. On the screen was a paused video of a car on a racetrack. I imagined the car was the fancy

Camaro he was picking up the following week. Steve wouldn't shut up about the damned thing.

"I'm driving," I said.

"This is it setting that time on the Nürburgring. That track in Germany that I was talking about."

"I'll look later," I said.

Steve grumbled, pulled his phone back, and watched the video.

I looked at the passing homes as we drove. While the houses weren't huge or new, each road jutting off to our right was bordered by canals that led straight into Biscayne Bay. I could see the bay itself at the end of each block. The homes had to cost a few million or more—probably getting close to ten for the larger or remodeled ones.

"That's our street there," Steve said. He pointed out the windshield at the approaching road and jammed his phone into his pocket. I slowed and made the turn down the dead-end street—Ocean Mist Court. A barricade, North Miami PD patrol cars, unmarked cruisers, and a county coroner's van were at the end of the block. We'd found our scene. To my left and right, the homes got progressively larger the closer to the end of the street we got. I slowed as we reached the uniformed officer at the makeshift barricade—a string of yellow police tape attached to two orange cones. The North Miami PD officer approached, and I dropped my window. The officer, wearing a dark-blue uniform, looked in at Steve and me.

"Homicide?" he asked.

He obviously didn't recognize us as being from his

department, thus his educated guess. "Yeah," I said. "Lieutenant Harrington and Sergeant Walsh." I showed my badge.

"I'll move the tape," the officer said. "She's getting a little crowded back in here. Park where you can."

"Thanks," I said.

The officer left the window and grabbed one of the cones that the police tape was attached to. We passed through. The dead-end street was clogged with cars and people. Only two homes took up the end of the block, one to the left and one to the right. Judging by the officers rummaging about to my left, I imagined that was the property. The home sat behind a chain-link fence and looked to be a full reconstruction as opposed to a remodel. It was the biggest property in the neighborhood. A portable green toilet sat just inside the fence, creating what I imagined was a nice eyesore for the neighbors across the street.

I found a place to park next to another unmarked cruiser. Steve and I stepped from the car and approached the house.

The three-story home was flat-roofed and modern in design. A concrete stairwell, beside a pair of two-car-garage voids with no doors, rose to the glass-and-concrete second level. Stickers were on what I figured were all new windows. The third level featured more windows but had large sections that were white-painted stucco. Scaffolding took up the entire left side of the home. There was no landscaping, just piles of dirt. We passed through the open chain-link fence and caught the attention of a man in a suit, who was standing near one of the garage voids with a uniformed North Miami patrol officer.

"Homicide?" the guy in the suit asked.

"Lieutenant Nash Harrington," I said. "Sergeant Steve Walsh," I added while jerking my head toward Steve.

"Alonso Huizenga, detective at North Miami," he said with a handshake.

"So, the word is we have two bodies," I said.

"Put out to be found, it looks like. Both men seem to have taken rounds center mass. The shooting didn't happen here as far as we can tell."

"Who found the bodies?" I asked.

"A woman from a landscape design company. One second." Huizenga fished into the breast pocket on his uniform and produced a business card, which he passed to me. "That's her. We checked with her office, and this place has been on their schedule for a couple weeks."

I had a look at the business card and the name—an Emily Karlsson, from Tropical Design and Solutions.

"Apparently the woman was called out to have a look at the grounds and draw up some kind of design and quote."

"Where is she?" I asked.

"After an hour or so of us checking her out and getting everything answered, we sent her on her way. I told her we'd follow up if we needed to."

I pulled out my phone and snapped a photograph of the business card before passing it back to Huizenga.

"All right. Where are the bodies?" I asked.

"In the back, on the dock." He started toward the side of the house.

Huizenga led us to the back of the property on the bay.

The lot was rounded, taking up the northeast corner of the peninsula the street was on. Freshly planted queen palms stood every twenty feet, wrapping the property—their fronds swayed in the breeze. The home's rear pool and entertaining area followed the curvature of the lot's seawall. Another man in a suit and two uniformed officers huddled around a blue tarp on the boat dock to our left. We walked over, and the smell of decomp grew with each step forward.

"Damn," Steve said, walking a few feet behind me.

I glanced back, and he'd covered his nose and mouth with the sleeve of his suit jacket.

Huizenga led us to the tarp, and the officers who were standing around it spread out so we could get our view. Huizenga crouched and pulled the tarp back. The two bodies lay faceup. Both men wore suits. The one on the left was slim with longer hair. His eyes were open, milky-white and fixed on me. The one on the right was overweight and bald. His eyes were closed, but his tongue protruded from his mouth. Both men were bloated and gray—dead for over twenty-four hours, I figured. The tarp had been pulled back far enough to reveal a pair of entrance wounds on the upper left side of the thin one's chest. I took a couple of steps to my left and stared down at the face of the longer-haired one. He looked familiar, too familiar to dismiss. My eyes went to the bald one beside him.

"Damn," I said. "I need to make a call."

"Recognize one of them?" Steve asked.

"Both of them. Just give me a second." I got upwind of the bodies and dialed the station. I had the receptionist put me through to Tillerson's desk in Vice.

"Tillerson," he answered.

"It's Harrington," I said.

"Hey, what's up?"

"I think I have something bad here. What's the name of the slim, long-haired undercover that you have? Works with a shorter bald guy? The two that picked up that prostitute for questioning for me a couple months back while we were working the Clifford Walton case."

"It sounds like you're talking about Frost and Nance," he said. "Why?"

"Do you know where they are?" I asked.

"Why?" he asked. The single word was filled with worry.

"We got called out to a scene. There's two bodies. And unfortunately, a resemblance," I said.

Silence came from his end of the call—too much of it.

"You there?" I asked.

Tillerson let out a big breath, which was followed by some muffled cursing. I gave him a second.

"How much of a resemblance?" Tillerson asked. "Is it them?"

"Enough of a resemblance for me to call," I said.

"Son of a bitch," Tillerson said. "Frost and Nance were supposed to check in almost a week ago," he said. "They never did. Frost's wife called yesterday saying that she hadn't heard anything from Frost in days and was getting concerned. I tried reaching out to both of them. I got nothing."

"Sorry, Tillerson. I think I found them," I said.

He cursed again, paused, and let out another hard breath. "Where are you?"

"Some under-construction house in North Miami."

"On Ocean Mist Court?"

"Yeah. You know the house?"

"Frost was using it for something we were working on."

"Which was what?" I asked.

"It's a long story." Tillerson again released a puff of air into the phone. "What was the COD?"

"GSWs."

Tillerson said he was on his way and clicked off before I had time for another word.

"These guys some of ours?" Steve asked, walking up.

I slid my phone back into my pocket. "If they're who I think, they worked undercover in Vice."

"How sure are we that this is what we're dealing with?" Steve asked.

"Tillerson lost contact with both guys and knew of this house. Pretty damn close to a hundred percent."

"Damn," Steve said. "All right. What are we doing here? Is Tillerson on his way?"

"Yeah. I'm sure we'll get more as soon as he shows up. Until then, let's get to banging on doors and talking with the neighbors. These houses, in this kind of neighborhood, someone is going to have some video security somewhere."

"Got it," Steve said. He left my side and started rounding up officers.

I stared at the tarp that had been laid over the two men. Someone left them there to be found. The wind stirred up and sent more of the decomp smell in my direction. I turned and headed for the front of the house. I needed to know what exactly our vice guys had been sniffing around in.

CHAPTER 3

I'd just gotten a text from Tillerson saying he'd been on scene for a few minutes, so I fired off a reply that we were next door talking to the neighbors and would be back shortly. I stuffed my phone into my pocket and returned my attention to the gray-haired female homeowner, Carol Thompson. "So how much of the water do your cameras capture?" I asked.

We stood by the seawall at the edge of her property. A six-foot-tall white fence wrapped the property line and separated her yard from the scene next door. The fence hadn't blocked Mrs. Thompson as she watched from a spare bedroom window while the scene unfolded all morning. She'd seen the tarp and, from what she'd said, got a view of the bodies through her binoculars when the tarp was pulled back.

She jerked her chin toward the water. "It captures the entire channel here," she said. "We had some people a few years back that stole some little statues off our dock and rummaged through our boat. After that, my husband had the surveillance system put in." She turned toward her house and pointed at the camera attached to the top corner of the second story. "That one there catches all of our dock, the water, and almost all of each of the neighbor's docks as well. It's high enough where the fence isn't an issue. I'd say if someone tied up a boat next door, or did much of anything on the dock, our cameras should have caught it."

"What about the front?" I asked. "Do your cameras cover the street as well?"

"Just in front of the house. We have one above our garage door."

"Okay," I said.

"And you said your husband will be home soon?" Steve asked.

"Yeah. If I knew how to work the equipment, I'd just show you, but it's probably easier if we wait on Gary than have him try to coach me or one of us through it while he's driving."

"All right," I said. "Did you see anything going on next door prior to this morning? Maybe a car or some people you didn't recognize?"

"There are always different cars, trucks, and people over there. Some are workers, some are from the realty office, some are unknowns," she said.

"When was the last time you saw someone over there?" I asked.

"Yesterday, actually. A van," she said. "I don't think I saw any of the workers, but I think it was commercial. Before that, it was probably a week or more. But that's just what I saw. Obviously, there could have been people there that I didn't see."

"Okay," Steve said. "Do you happen to remember a company name or anything on that van?"

"Sorry," she said.

A noise caught my ear from the back of the woman's house. I turned to see a man, thin and of a similar age as Mrs. Thompson, come from a sliding patio door.

"That's Gary, my husband," she said.

The man was dressed in tan shorts and a tucked-in polo shirt. He wore a golf-brand baseball cap and had a white sweater draped over his shoulders. He looked as if he'd just come from a country club, which was fitting since he had.

"It was like pulling teeth to get the police out front to let me through so I could pull into the driveway." He stepped from the porch and walked across the yard to Steve, me, and his wife.

"Gary Thompson," he said while holding out his hand for a handshake.

I shook the guy's hand and introduced myself and Steve.

"What the hell happened over there?" he asked. "I'm trying to get a round of golf in and Carol calls me and says she saw bodies on the dock next door. Cops everywhere."

"That's basically what we've got," I said. Trying to pretend it was anything else would have been wasting time. The man could simply walk in his house and look at the scene next door to see exactly what was going on.

"Why the hell would there be bodies dropped on the dock at an empty house?" His brow furrowed. "This isn't the kind of thing that happens in this neighborhood."

I didn't have enough information—or any, really—on

just what Vice was doing in connection with the house, so I couldn't answer his questions.

"We can't really speculate about what happened until we gather some more information. Which is what brought us over. Your wife says that you've got video surveillance that captures the front and back? Maybe some of the neighboring home's dock over there that we could look at?"

"We've got video surveillance," he said. "You guys are more than welcome to see what it caught."

Steve and Mrs. Thompson began to follow the husband. Before I could take a step, I felt my phone buzz. I pulled it out to see another text from Tillerson, which was confirming that the deceased men were Frost and Nance. Steve could handle watching the video and dealing with the neighbors. I wanted to hear from Tillerson what kind of operation Vice had been running and who they'd been running it on.

"Hey, Steve."

He turned and paused.

"Tillerson is next door. I'm going to go have a talk with him. You got this?"

"Yeah," Steve said. "I'll let you know what we get."

I thanked the Thompsons, headed along the side of their house to the front of the property, then went next door to the scene. I didn't spot Tillerson out front—he was seated on a concrete bench in a backyard that looked out over the bay. Holding a phone to his ear, Tillerson glanced over his shoulder at me as I walked up.

"I'm going to have to go to Frost's house," Tillerson said. He took the phone from his ear and set it beside him on the bench. "And tell his wife. Nance was single, but he's got a brother and mother that are local."

I stood in the grass between the bench and seawall and looked down at Tillerson. The collar of his dress shirt was unbuttoned, and his tie had been loosened. He looked at me and put his fingers through his mussed, mostly gray hair. Tillerson's weathered face showed a mix of anger and grief. He shook his head and fished a cigarette from a pack that he'd pulled from his inner suit jacket pocket. "I just got off the phone with some of my guys. I asked them to go out to the house Frost had been staying in and the house where Nance had been. We'll see what I hear back." Tillerson lit his smoke and sucked in a big drag.

"What the hell were these guys working on?" I asked.

Tillerson exhaled a cloud of smoke from his nostrils. "Someone is flooding the streets with Krokodil," he said. "It's spreading like a disease."

"I've heard of it, but give me a refresher," I said.

"Synthetic opioid. Ten times stronger than morphine but only lasts a short duration—maybe two hours, max. Hits like a dump truck and then disappears just as fast. Withdrawal is on the level of heroin, so people constantly need their fix. Highly, highly profitable for whoever is making and distributing it."

"Doesn't it mess with your skin or something. Scales or whatever? Taking the name into account."

"It rots flesh," Tillerson said. "Users get open ulcers and gangrene. Skin infections. Blood poisoning. Amputations are common if people are shooting veins in appendages.

21

That is, if they get treated at all. It's just some nasty stuff all the way around."

"Ugh," I grumbled. "Where the hell is it coming from?"

Tillerson shook his head. "We've been trying to work our way up the ladder, starting with the street dealers, but haven't been having too much luck. We've been trying to put something together to get beyond that street level and into distribution but have just kind of been spinning wheels. It seems local, but nobody is talking. Nobody knows anything. Hell, Mullin has been deep cover for years and didn't have anything for us when we reached out to him a few months back. All we know for certain is that it's not coming from the usual suspects."

"Mullin?" I interrupted. "Who is that?"

"Technically, he's a fed now. He was one of our undercover guys some time back that we still have a working relationship with." Tillerson took another drag of his cigarette and flicked the ash.

"All right. You can fill me in on him in a second. How is this house connected to this?" I asked.

"Frost was posing as a high-end real estate developer. Nance was posing as an associate of his. The house was a piece in that."

"Make the connection to the drugs for me," I said.

"We were putting the word on the streets that someone had a network for distribution to other states. The hopes were that we'd catch the ear of whoever was behind the Krokodil. The story was that Frost, posing as the real estate developer, had multiple properties on the water throughout the Miami area.

Product could be offloaded at or taken to any of the properties, reloaded, and then transported through an insured, self-contained network to wherever it needed to go. See, we don't know if it's coming in off the water or not, so doing it the way we did kind of covered both bases."

"Explain the self-contained-network thing," I said.

Tillerson took a pull from his smoke. "Basically, we were saying that if you brought it to one of these properties via boat or truck, we'd guarantee the shipment out of state and get it to where it needed to go."

"And why would someone look to go outside their organization for something like this and take up business with someone new?"

"A no-risk distribution channel is pretty damn hard to pass up. Plus, we had Mullin's help. With the four years that he's been deep cover, he's kind of established himself as part of the criminal community, if you will. He's been posing as a playboy millionaire that dabbles in a little bit of everything." Tillerson took a big final drag from his cigarette and flicked the butt into the water. I didn't lecture him on it. "He agreed, if asked, to say that he'd worked with Frost before. Basically, to vouch for Frost if anyone came asking."

"And did he?"

"I don't know. I'm going to request a phone call," Tillerson said. "Hopefully, he can call and give us some answers."

"Where is he?" I asked. "Someplace local where we can go and have a chat with him? Maybe send someone to pick him up?"

Tillerson shook his head. "That's not an option. We'd have the bureau's wrath to deal with. I'll reach out, and we'll see what we get."

"You said he's been undercover for almost four years. What the hell is he working on? A bachelor's?"

"Originally, when he was with us, we had him undercover working a drug case that we thought a local family was involved in."

"Family as in mob?"

"Yeah. Mullin buddied up with this guy named Moretti, and it turned out that Moretti was someone that the feds had a lot of interest in. The bureau swooped in, basically told Mullin he now reported to them, and told Vice to cease and desist whatever we were working. All they wanted Mullin to do was keep sending info down the pipeline. They finally had their in, even if he was a vice UC and not one of their own."

"He turned into their golden boy," I said.

"Yeah he did. They gave him everything he needed to establish his cover. And then about a year or so in, Moretti disappeared off the face of the earth. Mullin wanted out. The feds, however, didn't want to let him go. He'd gotten in with a lot of people and had become an irreplaceable asset. They needed him to maintain his cover and keep feeding them intel. I guess they worked out some kind of deal because they took Mullin off our books. It's been three years now that he's been with them."

"Well, we need to talk to him," I said. "And I need whatever you have on Frost and Nance. Real home addresses, false of the same. Everything on their cover identities. Associates, family members for both guys. Everything."

"I'll get it all to you today." Tillerson rose from the bench. "I have to go and make this house call. I don't want Frost's wife finding out from someone else. I'll call you as soon as I have everything put together for you."

CHAPTER 4

Manny

As Manny walked to Matt, he saw Justin leaning against the pool bar, staring up at the television. Matt was seated under an umbrella at a poolside patio table, drinking a mimosa and eating from a plate of grapes and cheese. "They found them," Manny said. "I drove past this morning. The whole street was filled with cops."

"Good," Matt said.

Manny stepped under the shade of the umbrella to get out of the morning sun. Sitting on the table was the file that they'd retrieved the day before from the house of the fat cop, Nance.

"What do you want to do about that?" Manny asked. He jerked his chin at the file.

"Nothing to do. And not enough in here to worry about," Matt said. "What those two told me was the extent of it. They don't have any names other than Tavaras. And he, one, doesn't know anything, and two, will be dead shortly."

"It mentions the carpet-cleaning businesses, though.

How the hell would Tavaras even know about that?"

"Someone said something. Maybe one of the guys at the businesses. Either way, it didn't sound like either of the cops knew anything."

"How do we know that there isn't another file?" Manny asked.

"Because they told me there wasn't another. Nowhere in this file does it mention the business by name. And I doubt the police are going to get search warrants for every carpet-cleaning business in the city. We'd hear about it if they did. And if a warrant had our business name on it, we'd get a heads-up."

Manny let out a hard breath.

"You guys went top to bottom on these guys' places, right? This file was it? Right where I told you it would be?"

"The file was right where you said it would be, yeah. Eric and Paul said all they found was the couple grand in cash, which was passed up to you, and that file. No computers, no folders, no memory sticks, no nothing. As far as the houses they were staying at, there was nothing on us. Nothing on you. I don't think it would be a bad idea if we looked into their true identities further and see if they—"

"Nah," Matt said, interrupting. "I'll make a couple phone calls myself and see where we're at. No messing with the cop's families."

Manny didn't respond. He rubbed at his eye.

Matt stared up at him. "What?"

"Nothing," Manny grumbled.

"Obviously, you still have a problem. Spit it out," Matt said.

"Just the whole damn thing. The cops, the file, leaving two dead cops to be found. It's not how we do things."

"Really?" Matt's tone indicated that he wasn't pleased with being questioned.

"Look, I don't want you to take it the wrong way, but that didn't seem like the best idea to me. We should have just sunk the pricks and been done with it."

"Now you know what's best for running my business?" Matt asked. "Now you're telling me how we do things? Your job is to do what I tell you. If you can't do that, maybe you're not the right person for what I need."

Whether the words were spoken directly or not, Manny knew Matt well enough to know he'd just been threatened. And while Manny normally felt free to voice his opinion, even if it led to an argument, it seemed like something had changed. Manny felt he needed to tread lightly and defuse the situation. "I'm not trying to tell you how to run anything. I'm not stupid, and I know my role here. It's just, you know, they'll have a forensic team going over every inch of everything. Some stupid piece of sand or something could lead them back to this property."

Matt chuckled. "A piece of sand is going to lead them to this house?"

"You know what I mean," Manny said. "I just think it was an unnecessary risk. What we've been doing has been working a hundred percent. Make it, send it, collect the money. Anyone gives us a problem or starts to get loose lips, they get popped and sunk. Not one person has come back up from the bottom of the bay. Everything has been clean until now. Were the cops supposed to be some kind of message or something?"

"Manny, that wasn't a message," Matt said. "That was part of a negotiation. That was me being a man of my word."

"What are you talking about?"

"Okay. Let me spell this out, because it doesn't sound like you're going to shut up about it until I do. I told them that I knew they were cops. That they were dead. That their families were dead. I told the one what I'd do to his wife. I told the other what would happen to his mother. I gave them a choice. Tell me everything and it would just be them. I would leave their bodies to be found so their families could get their pensions. So they wouldn't be declared missing and be denied insurance and pension money for years. I told them it would be clean, in the chest so they could have open caskets. I told them if I found out they were lying to me after I killed them, I would go back after their families. We made a deal, and their words have been truthful to this point. Now, what about the boat?" Matt asked. "You took it to Roger?"

Manny said nothing. He was trying to process how everything could have gone down in the shed. How that much negotiating could have been discussed. Matt had been inside with the men for only a few minutes.

"The boat?"

"Ah, yeah, we dropped it with him at the marina this morning," Manny said. "He said that the boat itself will be stripped and the hull destroyed as soon as he can get to it. The motor is going to get used on something else that we can pick up over there in a few days. Similar setup, though."

"Good," Matt said. "And how are we doing on finding Tavaras? He needs to be dealt with sooner rather than later."

"I sent Paul and Eric out looking for him. The word is he has a couple of places, so they're checking around."

"All right. Everything is as it should be. Sit. Eat some of this. You want Justin to make you a drink or something?"

"I'm good," Manny said.

"Soda? Tea? Water?"

"I'm good. Thank you," Manny said. "Where's Frank?"

"He's out doing some errands." Matt pointed at the chair across from him at the table. "Sit. You're making me nervous."

Manny slid out the chair and plopped down. "What's on the agenda for today?"

"We need to go see Jaime," Matt said as he tossed a grape in his mouth. "Probably around two o'clock."

"See him where?" Manny asked.

"He'll be at the store off 103rd today. I'd like to pop in on him."

Matt usually didn't make personal appearances. He stayed out of sight, in the shadows. Frank rarely left the compound either. If a problem needed to be dealt with, Manny, serving as lieutenant, would normally handle it with the help of Eric and Paul. "I'll take care of it. What do you need?" Manny asked.

Matt waved his hand. "I need to show my face there."

"Okay. But what's the reason for the visit? Jaime seems to be running a pretty tight ship over there."

"He's a bit slow on collecting money owed. Plus,

something has been brought to my attention that I need to speak with him about. Call the visit a performance review."

Manny shrugged. "Sure. Whatever." He wiped some sweat from his forehead. While the umbrella over the table filtered the sunlight hitting him in the face, the temperature was quickly rising through the eighties. A cool drink might be just what he needed. "You know, screw it. I will have that drink."

"Justin!" Matt shouted. "Make Manny a drink."

CHAPTER 5

Skip arrived on scene and, after Colt photographed everything, removed the bodies. Gomez had been working his way through the home itself. While the place had been locked up, and we didn't have anything to suggest anyone had been inside, it wouldn't go unchecked.

The video from the Thompson home next door to our scene didn't give us a ton. Though they'd said their cameras caught a good portion of the neighbor's dock, the footage didn't include the portion we needed—the portion the bodies were on. While the bodies could have been brought to the house and placed on the dock via land, the more logical conclusion was that someone had pulled up with them in a boat. Steve and I had been door knocking every house on both sides of the canal. We were at the end of the block, at the last house directly across the canal from our scene.

We walked up the driveway toward the light-gray home. The house was one that appeared to have had a top-to-bottom makeover and, by the looks of the nontraditional roofline, an addition as well. The garage sat adjacent to a recessed front entryway. Short shrubs cut into perfect squares followed the sidewalk to the double front doors.

I pressed the bell and gave the door a few raps with my fist. A moment later, the door pulled open. A man with black-framed glasses, somewhere in his fifties, gave Steve and me a nod.

"Police, right?" he asked.

"I'm Lieutenant Nash Harrington. This is Sergeant Steve Walsh," I said, pointing at Steve.

"Roger Monroe. I've been watching the commotion across the canal for the last hour or so. I saw the bodies on the dock."

I didn't have a response for him.

"Mr. Monroe, we were just checking with the surrounding homes, looking to see if anyone witnessed anything or happened to have any security cameras that may catch the canal," Steve said.

"Yeah," he said. "And it's good that you guys are here. I was about to go stand in my backyard and try to wave someone over."

"Security video?" I asked. "Or saw what happened?"

"I wasn't home overnight but went to my cameras after I saw all that going on over there. I pulled up what you guys are probably looking for. A boat came up, and a couple of guys offloaded the bodies around three in the morning."

"Can we get a look?" I asked.

"Yeah. We need to head back to my office," he said. "Come in."

Steve and I followed the homeowner inside and through

his house. The entire place had been renovated in a modern design. What wasn't white was gray, making for a rather sterile and stark-looking interior. Mr. Monroe appeared to be the only one there. After we passed a big kitchen and living room, he led us through a pair of open French doors to a large home office. The desk faced us, and behind it were bookshelves filled with photos and achievement plaques—from where I stood, I couldn't tell what they were for. The office sat at the back of the home and had a view of the canal through the pool cage. On the far side of the water was the scene and the officers milling about.

Mr. Monroe took a seat at his desk and all but disappeared behind a huge computer monitor. A second after he sat down, his head poked out from the side of it. "If you guys want to come around to this side, you can have a look," he said.

Steve and I rounded the guy's desk and got a view of what was on the computer screen.

"The footage isn't the best, but you can pretty clearly see what is going down," he said.

Mr. Monroe played the footage, and Steve and I stood behind him and watched the computer screen. The monitor looked to be positioned somewhere to the left of the pool cage and pointed toward his dock. Beyond the dock belonging to the property, moonlight bounced off the waters of the canal and the under-construction home across the canal—where our murder happened. The bottom of the corner video monitor showed the time and date—a few minutes before three that morning, just as the homeowner had said.

A few seconds of nothing played until the bow of a bay

boat came into frame. The boat had a big single motor, dark exterior, and a white deck. A tower rose from the center console. There appeared to be three men on it—the one piloting the boat and two who were seated. The guy at the controls looked wide for his height. All the men appeared to be wearing baseball caps. From the distance and darkness, we wouldn't be able to make out any identifying details about them. The same could be said for the boat—it was too far away from the camera to get any registration number or make—though I hoped that maybe Wade in our tech unit could work a little magic with the footage.

The boat floated up to the dock, and the seated men rose. Both men were taller than the pilot. One of the guys quickly tied up a rope, and the other jumped onto the dock. Within seconds, they had both bodies off the boat and in the spots where we'd found them. I watched the one guy hop back down into the boat, the other untied it, and a moment later, the group shoved off and disappeared off camera.

"That was pretty smooth. Pretty damn efficient," Steve said.

"What do you suppose Nance, the bigger of the two, weighed? He had to be damn near two hundred fifty pounds," I said. "Those two guys had him up and off that boat like he weighed nothing."

"They didn't look little," Steve said. "Probably muscle for whoever is behind this."

I nodded but said nothing.

"What time were the bodies found this morning?" Steve asked.

"I'm not sure exactly," I said. "Can we get you to fast-forward what your cameras caught up to this morning?" I asked Mr. Monroe.

The homeowner nodded without turning back toward Steve and me. With a couple of clicks of his computer mouse, the footage on the screen sped up. The time stamp at the bottom of the screen spun up to roughly eight thirty in the morning when we spotted movement.

"There," I said. "Let's rewind a bit and then play that."

Mr. Monroe did as I asked. We sat and watched as what I figured was the woman from the landscape company wandered into the backyard. She held what looked like a clipboard and walked slowly as she appeared to take notes. After a minute or two in the back, she took a meandering course for the dock, stopped dead in her tracks, and dropped the clipboard. She ran to the front yard. Minutes passed without anyone appearing on screen.

"You want me to fast-forward until we see something?" Mr. Monroe asked.

"Please," I said.

He did, and under ten minutes later, a pair of uniformed officers appeared in the backyard. We watched as they got a look. One of the guys appeared to immediately go for his shoulder radio.

"Can we go back to the drop?" Steve asked.

"Yeah, sure," Mr. Monroe said.

He brought up the footage, and we watched it again. Nothing called for immediate action.

"All right. What do we have to do to get a copy of this from you?" I asked.

"Um," Mr. Monroe said. "I'm pretty sure that I can plug in some kind of memory stick to transfer the video to. I don't know—I've never had to do it. I'd have to find the manual or call the place that I got it from."

"We've got a tech guy who could come out and take care of it if it's okay with you," I said.

"Yeah, that's fine," Mr. Monroe said. "No work for me today."

"Sounds good. We'll make the call and send him over as soon as he gets here. He'll be a bald guy named Wade."

"All right."

We thanked Mr. Monroe and left his house. Steve made the call to Wade as we headed around the block to the scene. As we turned the corner onto Ocean Mist Court, the coroner's van drove toward us. Colt was following in his truck. I gave Skip in the van a wave as he passed, and I flagged Colt to stop for a quick word. I went to the window of his truck.

Colt tucked some of his long blond hair under his forensics ball cap. "I'm headed to the ME's office," he said. "Try to get a better look at these two there. Gomez was just finishing up with the house. Did you guys get anything?"

"Video of the drop from the property directly across the canal," I said.

Colt threw the truck into Park. "How did it go down?"

"About as smoothly as possible," I said. "Three guys in a bay boat pulled up. Two of them offloaded the bodies, hopped back on, and took off. I'd say a minute from pull up to cast off."

"Never touched the house?" Colt asked.

"Never touched land. A couple of steps on the dock and that was it." My phone vibrated in my pocket. I slid it out far enough to see the screen. It was my mother—I'd have to call her back.

"Anything on the video to ID the guys?" Colt asked.

"The pilot was wide and looked about average size," I said. "The other two who unloaded the bodies looked big. Probably mid six-foot range and mid two-hundred-pound range. Too far away and too dark to really get any more than that."

"What about the boat?" Colt asked.

"Single-engine bay boat. About all we can tell without doing something with the video. Steve is on the line with the tech unit to get Wade out here. Maybe he can get something more."

Colt appeared to be in thought. "Was there a tower on the boat?" he asked.

"Yeah."

"If we can nail down the make and model of the boat, we can use the dimensions of the tower to help with our guys' approximate heights and weights. It's something."

"Wade is on his way," Steve said. He walked up beside me next to Colt's passenger window.

"Good," I said. "How long do you think you'll be at the ME's office, Colt?"

"I don't know. An hour or two," Colt said. "Depends on what we find."

"All right. We'll let you catch up to Skip. Give me a ring if you get something," I said.

"Will do," Colt said.

CHAPTER 6

"So that's where we're at," I said.

Captain Halloway, leaning against my office doorjamb with his arms crossed over his chest, grunted a response.

My phone buzzed against my leg. I slid it out and had a look at the screen. My mother was calling again. I remembered that she'd called earlier, but I hadn't had a chance to call her back—I would as soon as Halloway and I finished our talk. I tossed my phone onto my desk. It continued to buzz.

"Need to take that?" Halloway asked.

"It's just my mom. I'll call her back."

"Maybe something is wrong. Take it," he said.

"I assure you nothing is wrong. I'll give her a buzz back in a minute."

"All right. When is Tillerson giving you everything he's got on these two?" Halloway asked.

"I just talked to him a few minutes ago. He was on his way back from Frost's house, where he'd given the news to Frost's wife. Her name is Christine."

Halloway rubbed the back of his neck. "Damn."

"Yeah. Not good," I said.

"What about the other one? Nance? Any local family?" the captain asked.

"Tillerson said a mother and brother that were local."

"Their vehicles?"

"Waiting on Tillerson," I said. "All he gave me was the pair of addresses they were staying at under their assumed names. I have Garcia and Ryan working on the assumed names to get me whatever they can."

"All right. You said you wanted to round everyone up in the conference room once Tillerson gets in?"

"I'm thinking that's probably going to be the easiest. He can give everyone what he knows, what these guys were working on. They can ask their questions instead of me going back and forth. We'll get everything from Tillerson and then start dividing it up. Start checking things off the list. The main thing is getting out to where these guys were staying and having a look around. Tillerson said that their places had been tossed."

"Tossed, huh?"

"Yeah. I guess he sent one of his other vice guys out there to check on the homes. Both ransacked."

"Who was looking for what?"

"Good question," I said.

My desk phone rang.

"Okay. Grab me when Tillerson gets in," Halloway said.

"Sure." I reached for my phone, and the captain left my office. I had a pretty good idea who was calling.

"Harrington," I answered.

"Hey, I tried your cell phone, but you didn't answer. A

couple times. I even left a message on your answering machine. I figured I'd try your desk. Your dad told me not to bug you, but I just had a quick question."

The last few days, my mother had had "a quick question" about ten times a day. My parents had decided that they wanted to come for a visit. It had been going on a year since they'd come down from Mt. Dora, and while I'd seen them probably ten times in that span, it was always me making the drive up to them. "What do you need, Mom?"

"I just need to know where you keep the shortening," she said.

The hollow, almost echoing sound accompanying her words led me to believe I was on Speaker. "I don't have any," I said.

The sound of my kitchen cabinet doors opening and closing came through the phone. "Are you sure?" she asked.

"I'm positive."

"Okay. What about cream of tartar?"

"Cream of who?"

"Baking soda?" she asked.

"I don't have any of that kind of stuff."

I heard her grumble and another cabinet door close.

"What are you trying to do, Mom?" I asked.

"She's trying to make snickerdoodles," my father shouted, confirming my suspicion of being on Speaker.

"Anything that you'd need for baking, you'd have to get from the store," I said.

"Well, how does Amy bake anything?"

I leaned back in my chair and looked at my office ceiling.

"That's fine. I'll have your father run me to the store. Lucky is almost out of treats, anyway," she said.

"I just picked her up a bag yesterday. They're in the pantry next to the fridge."

"Yeah, it's empty."

"That was probably the old bag. I just bought a new one. It's not even open."

"Blue bag with a cartoon dog on the side?" my mom asked.

"Yeah, that's it," I said.

"That's the one that's empty."

"Tell me that you didn't feed my dog a bag of dog treats in a day."

"She was doing tricks. And then we went on a walk and were at the park," she said.

I let out a long breath but said nothing. The older my parents got, the more patience I needed. I assumed it was the world paying me back for what I did to them in my teenage years.

"Okay. We're going to run to the store," my mother said. "I'll call you if I need anything."

"Sure," I said.

"Love you, sweetie." She hung up.

I reached out, set the phone back on its base, and glanced out of my office window. Steve, Ryan, and Garcia were all seated at their desks. I left my office and walked out to the bull pen. I'd asked the guys to dig in on the little information that we had.

Steve glanced up at me as I approached. "I've been trying

to find anything similar," he said. "I found some cases where Krokodil and Russian organized crime were mentioned together but nothing with any killing of undercovers. Yet for some reason, if this is tied to one of the Russian cliques, maybe our ol' colleague Ivan could help us out."

Miami had a bit of a Russian mob problem, so it wasn't out of the question that the murders might be related. The mob had even infiltrated our department in years past. The Ivan that Steve spoke of was former Sergeant Ivan Blok. As it turned out, in addition to being in law enforcement, he was also connected to a Russian organized crime syndicate run by two brothers, Ray and Viktor Azarov. When some friends from the Tampa PD were finally able to bring the Azarovs down, Sergeant Blok's involvement was revealed. The former sergeant was currently serving a sentence for a slew of charges, including conspiracy to commit murder. He wouldn't be stepping foot outside of prison as a free man anytime soon. How he could help us—or if he would—I didn't know. Yet if the investigation stalled, it might be worth trying to talk to him.

"We'll rattle his cage if we need to," I said. "Let's wait and see what we get from Tillerson."

Steve nodded. "I'm going to make a call over to the bureau too. Maybe they've seen something that isn't out in the public."

"Good idea," I said. I turned my attention to Ryan, a desk over from Steve. "Anything?"

"I pulled their sheets," Ryan said. "Or fake sheets or cover sheets or whatever you want to call them. They look pretty good. Nothing that screams fake. Neither shows any significant time served. Just a couple-month stretch at a minimum security on Frost, or Winter as he was going by." He pulled the papers from his desk and held them out. As I took them from Ryan, Garcia stood from his desk and joined us.

"We need Tillerson to give us something to actually work with," Garcia said.

"One second," I said.

I looked over the rap sheets for the identities that Nance and Frost had been using. Frost's was on top. He was going by the name Ken Winter. He had just two charges, both a few years old and both for wire fraud. He received a year at a white-collar facility for the offense—and he'd only served four months, which was about right. The address listed on his sheet was the same as Tillerson had given me. Registered vehicles were a Mercedes and a Ferrari. Both vehicles were just a few years old, and I imagined both came from the city's impound lot. The history looked pretty damn spot-on for someone posing as a crooked real estate developer.

I flipped a couple of pages until I had Nance's information before me. It appeared he was going by the name Aaron Kraft. His sheet showed a DUI and possession charge from two years prior. That was it. The listed address, just like Frost's, rang a bell as one that Tillerson had given me. Registered vehicles were a pair of Porsches.

"Let's get BOLOs on all four vehicles," I said. I passed the papers back to Ryan.

"Do we know that the cars aren't at the addresses here?" he asked and waved the sheets of paper.

"Don't know. Let's just do it, and if the vehicles are spotted at the homes, they're spotted at the homes," I said.

"Got it." Ryan reached for the phone at his desk.

"Geez," Steve said.

I glanced over at him as he furrowed his brow and tapped away at his computer keyboard.

"You want to see some gruesome photos, try giving that drug a search," he said.

I didn't need to. I knew well enough what the drug did, and after seeing two bloated bodies on the dock that morning, seeing flesh rotting off drug users wasn't high on my list of things to do.

"So, Vice thinks that this was some kind of new organization?" Garcia asked.

"I guess," I said.

"What made them think that?" he asked.

I shrugged. "They crossed the usual suspects off the list somehow."

"Did these two, Frost and Nance, have some kind of contact?" Garcia asked. "Someone who was dealing it or something?"

"I don't know. We're going to have a little meeting as soon as Tillerson gets in. Hopefully we can get all of our questions answered quickly and get to work."

"Dispatch put the BOLOs out," Ryan said. He hung his phone up.

"Good," I said.

CHAPTER 7

Manny

Manny waited with his directional on to pull into the parking lot of the Gladeview carpet-cleaning business. Matt owned four of the businesses across the city. The big commercial building had a customer door and a small show floor at the front. The rear held a pair of garage doors for the vans to pull in and out of. While mostly a front, the facility also operated as a legitimate carpet-cleaning business for customers who happened to call or walk in. Yet the business was often backlogged. Only one of the vans at each place was outfitted with the equipment to do the jobs.

"You want me to have them get the door, so we can pull straight inside the building?" Manny asked.

In the passenger seat, Matt shook his head. "Just pull into the lot and park like you're a customer. They don't need a heads-up that we're here."

Manny pulled Matt's ten-year-old minivan into a parking spot and shut it off. A faint whiff of burning oil filled his nose. Matt had two very different fleets of vehicles—one he used and one he didn't. In one of the compound's garages sat two Lamborghinis, three Ferraris, a couple of classic muscle cars, assorted Rolls Royces and Bentleys, and a handful of five-year-old luxury SUVs. At least a dozen cars, yet not one of the flashy sports cars or luxury barges ever left the compound. A few million dollars in vehicles sat there in the dark, covered in dust. The only vehicles used were those randomly parked around the grounds. The vehicles mostly consisted of mini vans, econo boxes, and family sedans. The fleet made up the most vanilla selection of autos possible—and that was by design. Matt traveled under the radar. He wouldn't take a seat in a single vehicle that might ever draw a second look. He never sat in the back like he was being driven, and often he drove himself. He liked to blend in, to remain unseen. Why he had all the expensive vehicles in the first place, Manny didn't know. He'd been working for Matt for only a year, and Matt had never discussed his past in any detail.

Manny glanced over at Matt in the passenger seat.

"Did Eric or Paul get back to you about Tavaras yet?" Matt asked.

"They're still looking for him," Manny said.

"When they find him, have them soften him up a bit before bringing him back to the house."

"I think that was pretty much going to happen either way," Manny said.

"Make sure it does."

"All right," Manny said. He fired off a quick text to Paul with the orders. "Message sent."

E. H. REINHARD

Matt pulled the door handle and stepped from the van—Manny followed. Matt, dressed in a floral shirt, board shorts, and flip-flops, walked to the business's front door. He yanked it open to the chime of bells. Manny trailed him inside.

Manny saw a thin, mid-thirties man emerge from an office and step to the front counter. The guy wore a black polo shirt, slacks, and a baseball cap with the business's logo on it. A thin goatee wrapped the guy's mouth—it was Jaime, the man in charge of the day-to-day operations of the four carpet-cleaning businesses or, more accurately, Krokodil production and distribution centers. "Hey, how can I help…" Jaime's words faded when he saw who was in the storefront. "Oh. No one told me you guys were stopping in today."

"I know," Matt said. He looked over his shoulder at Manny. "Door and sign."

Manny turned the lock for the front door and, at Matt's request, pulled the string on the Open sign.

"What, uh, what's up?" Jaime asked.

"Nothing," Matt said. "Just stopping in to see how everything is going."

"Everything is fine. Ah, we were just getting one of the shipments set in the back. Did you want to have a look?"

"Yeah." Matt nodded. He motioned for Jaime to lead the way.

As they were about to pass the front counter, Manny snatched a candy bar from the small rack next to the cash register.

Matt stopped and gave him a disapproving look. "Are you going to pay for that?"

"Yeah," Manny said. "I was just getting my wallet."

"Sure you were," Matt said.

Manny held the candy bar in his teeth by the corner of the wrapper while he fished his wallet from his pocket.

"Ring him up," Matt said.

Jaime did, and Manny tucked the receipt and three singles into his wallet. He dropped the loose change and wallet into his pocket and unwrapped the candy bar as he walked. A metal door separated the office and storefront from the warehouse in the back. Jaime punched a six-digit code into the keypad and pulled the door open. The group filed through. Four vans, all with graphics for the business, sat with the rear doors open. A pair of guys unloaded duffel bags from one of the vans and appeared to be distributing them among the others. Both guys paused and looked over at Manny and Matt. They quickly looked away and went back to work. Another man, thin and balding, had his back to the group. He appeared to be writing something on a clipboard. The guy glanced over his shoulder, gave Manny and Matt a quick nod, and returned to the clipboard.

"Where's that going?" Matt asked.

"Clint's going to run this van up to Chicago later this week," Jaime said. "The other one is going to Oklahoma City. Two hundred kilos split evenly. Everything that was made this week."

"Two hundred?" Matt asked.

"Correct," Jaime said.

Matt headed to the back of a van and unzipped one of the duffel bags. He pulled out a brown paper–wrapped brick. "One kilo," he said. "We sell this for ten thousand bucks. There's two hundred here. That's two million dollars. Nine-tenths of that is profit." Matt turned the brick in his hand and admired it. "This is going to get cut five times before it hits the streets. Each of these kilos will be worth anywhere from fifty to a hundred grand." Matt tossed the brick back into the bag. "All for some dust that will do nothing more than eventually kill you."

The two guys who had been loading the vans, the man with the clipboard, and Jaime all stood at attention and listened to Matt. Manny took a big bite of the chocolate and caramel candy bar and chewed.

"How much money did we bring in this month, John?" Matt asked.

The guy with the clipboard flipped two pages and appeared to be searching for a number. He looked at Matt. "A little under four million. Not nearly what we could have," he said.

Confused, Manny glanced at Matt. He'd never seen the guy with the clipboard before, and how Matt knew him, Manny didn't know.

Matt took a seat on the van's rear bumper. "Not nearly what we could have," he repeated. "See, that's the kind of talk that concerns me. We have the facility, inventory, manpower, distribution network, and supplies to produce five hundred kilos a week. Why am I looking at less than half of what we're capable of?" Matt looked up and locked eyes with Jaime.

"It's not that easy," Jaime said.

"Enlighten me," Matt said.

Standing a few feet in front of Manny, Jaime used his hands as he spoke. "I mean, okay, sure, in a perfect world, we theoretically could produce that, but it's just not realistic," he said. "Getting enough codeine is what slows everything down. We can probably average around four, maybe four and a half at full capacity. But even then, it comes down to a supply and demand thing. Lately we've had to limit the cooks due to some difficulties in selling the product."

"Yeah, that's what I heard," Matt said.

"From?" Jaime asked.

Matt didn't respond.

"It was just this week. I'm sure we'll be back at a hundred percent next week. There just wasn't the demand."

"Wasn't the demand. For one of the cheapest and most addictive things ever to hit the streets," Matt said.

"I don't know. The users still prefer heroin. Even at the higher price. The dealers are saying that everyone is afraid of our products' side effects," Jaime said.

Matt smirked. "You expect me to believe that drug users are afraid of the side effects of doing drugs? You're serious? Meth users with no teeth and covered in scabs. Crackheads robbing and stealing just to get their next hit. People smoking bath salts and going insane. PCP users losing their shit and jumping out of windows. These are the people who are worried about Krokodil?"

"It's just what I heard," Jaime said.

Matt cracked his neck from one side to the other. "You

were done when you took it upon yourself to limit the cooks—to limit my income." He looked over at Manny. "Shoot this asshole."

Manny jammed the rest of the candy bar in his mouth and stuffed the wrapper in his pocket. He removed the gun from his shoulder holster, took a step forward, and pressed it to the back of Jaime's head. Feeling Jaime's tensed muscles through the pistol, Manny recalled his first kill in the Dominican Republic. He was thirteen years old when, at the request of his uncle Francisco, he killed Ramon Almeida for skimming some cocaine off the top of one of his uncle's shipments. Ramon and his son Rafael used to play baseball with Manny in a vacant patch of land near his uncle's business. Francisco had Ramon kneel before Manny and held Manny's little hand around the grip of the pistol. Manny remembered the pink mist that hung in the air. He remembered Rafael's scream. He remembered his uncle's laugh.

"Please," Jaime said. "Let's just think about this."

"You took it upon yourself to interfere with my earnings. You're dead." Matt snapped his fingers at Manny. "Do it."

Matt's orders snapped Manny back to the matter at hand, but Manny hesitated.

"Now," Matt said.

Manny squeezed the trigger. The sound of the shot bounced off the walls of the metal building. Jaime's body dropped. Blood from his head spilled across the cement.

Matt stood from his seated position at the back of the van. He put eyes on John. "We'll be doing a cash pickup tomorrow. Have everything set."

"We will," John said. He whistled to the men who'd been loading the van. "Clean this up."

The two men hustled to Jaime's body—one grabbed hands, the other feet.

Matt walked to Manny. "Let's go."

Manny holstered his weapon and followed Matt from the store.

"Who the hell is John?" Manny asked as soon as they got in the van.

"He plays cards with Frank. I guess he was telling Frank about Jaime limiting production. I had Frank bring John to me the other day. I asked him if what Frank had said was true—he confirmed. I just wanted to come here to hear Jaime's side of things with my own ears."

"I could have taken care of it had I known what was going on."

"You were dealing with the two cops. I needed you focused on that."

Manny nodded and started the van. He was concerned that Matt had left him out of the loop on the matter.

"So, you think this John can actually do a better job?"

Matt shrugged. "Jaime had to go," he said. "Everyone has a shelf life. His expired."

Manny didn't respond. He backed from the parking space and pulled from the lot. While Manny never had a hand in any of the financial aspects of the business, it was becoming clear that lately, Matt had been more and more focused on earnings. Why, Manny didn't know. Even with the limited production that Jaime had just lost his life over, the business was still making a fortune. Manny had a feeling that something might have been going on that he wasn't informed about. Matt's order to kill Jaime didn't seem like something he would have done a few months back. Manny glanced over at Matt. He couldn't get a read on him, but considering how things had been going, he wasn't going to inquire.

Matt locked eyes on Manny. "Never again make me ask you to do something twice," he said. He turned his head and looked out the window.

CHAPTER 8

"The boat is a Yellowfin 24 Bay," Wade said. "The registration numbers look like they were removed. I don't think you're going to have much luck there."

"How popular of a boat?" I asked.

"I wouldn't call the boat itself rare. From what I got from the video, it looks like this one has black upholstery and piping. That may be what you'll want to pass along to the marine unit."

"Black upholstery and piping," I said.

"Yeah, piping meaning the tubing of the tower. I can't imagine that there are a ton out on the water here that are configured in the same colors. You'll probably want them to focus around the Biscayne Bay area as well due to this not really being an open-water boat."

"Okay. Anything else?"

"I'm still working on getting approximate heights and weights on these guys. I need to hunt down some dimensions on the boat's tower. I'll shoot you a text when I get that."

"Appreciate it, Wade," I said.

"You got it."

I ended the call with Wade and immediately called our marine unit. I relayed the information to Sergeant D'Bruzzi. He said that he'd put it out to his guys on the water and call me directly if he heard anything back.

"You ready?" I asked as I slipped my phone into my pocket.

"Yeah, let's see what we find," Steve said.

I pushed open the driver's-side door of the cruiser and stepped out into the U-shaped stone-and-gravel driveway of the 1920s home where Frost had been staying. The Mediterranean-style house was covered in ivy. Orange awnings hung over the upper and lower windows that faced the street. Perfectly manicured flower gardens wrapped towering palm trees. A guesthouse stood toward the back corner of the grounds. The place had to be set on a half-acre or more of land. Just a block off the bay, the home cost somewhere in the couple million-dollar range, I imagined.

Steve let out a long whistle. "We need to get into undercover work."

"Remember the scene from this morning?" I asked.

"Yeah, maybe we don't," he said. "This is a sweet place, though."

"Tillerson said the side door was where whoever broke in made entry. Still open as far as he said." I swung the driver's door closed and went to the cruiser's trunk. I popped it open and pulled a pair of gloves from the box in the car's kit.

Standing at my shoulder, Steve gloved up as well. "Has Forensics been in here to have a look around?" he asked.

"No. So keep that in mind."

"Got it," he said.

I used my forearm to close the trunk lid, and we walked to the house. Tillerson had said the place had been ransacked, so I wasn't holding out a ton of hope that we were going to find something that would lead us somewhere. Steve and I went along the side of the home and stopped at the side entrance. My eyes went down to the splintered wood around the door catch. The jamb had clear pry bar marks on it. We knew that someone had broken in, yet I wasn't going to take the chance that they'd possibly come back for another look. I reached into my jacket for my service weapon and used my foot to push the door open. The hinges squealed as the door swung and clanked against the stopper. Steve and I entered what looked like a butler's pantry. We quickly passed through into the kitchen. A wrought-iron rack with pots and pans hung from the ceiling above a big marble island. The same marble was used on the countertops. Some of the dark wooden cabinet doors were open. The big stainless range door hung open too, and miscellaneous papers were scattered on the Spanish tile floor. We passed through the kitchen and into a large living room. A chair sat flipped over against the wall. The cushions had been removed from the couch and shredded. A few plants had been knocked over. No one was there.

Steve pointed at the next room and started toward it. I followed. A small sitting room sat off the side of the living room, which we quickly cleared. I trailed Steve down a short hallway, and after clearing a bathroom and a few closets, we made our way up to the second floor. The second story held four bedrooms and two bathrooms. Each bedroom had been destroyed—someone was looking for something. What, I hadn't a clue. The mattresses were off the bed frames and cut up. Drawers from chests and dressers had been dumped on the floor. Closet doors hung open, the contents inside scattered about. We cleared everything and headed downstairs.

"I don't even know where the hell we start looking for anything," Steve said. "This place is shredded."

"Let's clear the guesthouse and garage, then we'll come back and start going room to room." Steve followed me through the kitchen, the butler's pantry, and then outside. The guesthouse, albeit a quarter of the size of the main home, matched the home in design as well as its pried-open door. Steve and I quickly cleared the ransacked one-bedroom, one-bath outbuilding then walked the forty feet to the garage.

The side door of the garage, like the guesthouse and main house, looked to have been forced open. We entered, and I flipped on the lights.

The detached two-car garage had only one car inside—a black Ferrari California. Both doors of the car were open as was the trunk. The trunk held nothing—completely empty.

"One of the BOLOs, eh?" Steve asked.

"Yeah. The other was a Mercedes."

I holstered my weapon, went to the open driver's door of the car, crouched, and got a look inside. The interior was all black leather with yellow stitching. The car looked as if it had just come off the show room floor. To say that it was clean inside was an understatement. There wasn't a gum wrapper, receipt, piece of gravel, or speck of dirt to be found. I leaned in and looked under the driver's seat—nothing. Steve went to the passenger side of the car and found more of the same—zip. We had a quick look over the rest of the garage then returned to the main home.

Steve scooped up some of the papers that had been on the floor of the kitchen—junk mail addressed to Ken Winter. For a cover to go over with criminals, the tiniest details had to be considered and checked off. One of the first things taken care of was that change of address forms in the false name were submitted to the post office. An easy way to spot an undercover was to check the mailbox where the person said they lived. Everyone got junk mail—even would-be criminals. And if the person working undercover never got any mail addressed to them, that was an easy thing to spot. Steve tossed the mail on the kitchen island.

I ventured out to the living room while Steve remained in the kitchen looking around. I moved one torn-up couch cushion to the side, and then another. The drawers of the entertainment center stood open. I had a quick look—all empty. After looping around the couch, I was walking to the sitting room beside the living room when something caught my eye. Next to the knocked-over plant and in the dirt from the pot was a footprint as clear as day. How I'd missed it upon clearing the house, I didn't know—but there it was. I went for a better look.

"We got a footprint back here," I called.

I stared at the flat heel and flat forefoot marks pressed into the loose dirt—a dress shoe. I set my foot on a dirt-free tile beside the print. My shoe was a good couple of inches smaller than the print next to it. I wore a size eleven, so the print had to have been a fifteen or larger. The size of the men on the boat immediately registered in my head.

Steve emerged into the living room. "Footprint?"

"Yeah," I said and pointed down.

"Damn. What the hell size is that?" Steve did the same thing that I did and stuck his foot next to it.

"Big," I said. "I'm going to call Colt and see what he can do about getting someone out here. If Colt and Gomez are busy, we're going to need someone else." I pulled out my phone.

"Real quick," Steve said. "What year was that Mercedes? The other BOLO vehicle that Frost had."

"Sixteen, I think," I said.

"Let me make a call," Steve said. "I don't remember what the hell it's called, but Mercedes has some kind of tracking that comes with their newer cars. I was looking at one of the C-series AMG models, and the sales guy kept talking about all the stuff you could do with some app. Tracking the car was one of those things."

Steve made his call, and I dialed Colt. He answered after a few rings.

"Hey, I'm just leaving Skip at the ME's office," Colt said.

"And?" I asked.

"And I'm going to have to wait to get the bullets to run ballistics tests on, but there isn't much more than that. TOD is between twenty-four and forty-eight hours ago."

"That's a pretty big window," I said.

"It's what we have to work with right now."

"So, nothing with the bodies that could lead us anywhere?"

"Not that we found yet. Skip is going to do the autopsy on Frost, then Nance. He said he'd call me when the bullets have been removed from the bodies and I can get started with them."

"ETA on the autopsy reports?" I asked.

"Skip said this evening. I wish we would have found more, but there just wasn't anything to work with. What do you guys have out there?"

"A house that needs to be gone through. We've got a footprint in some dirt inside."

"Okay. Where's the house?"

"Bayshore. Just off Biscayne Boulevard," I said.

"All right. I'll call back to the station and loop around to meet you guys. I'm only about fifteen minutes away right now."

"Sounds good," I said.

CHAPTER 9

"Thanks," Steve said and ended his call. "The person I talked with at Mercedes customer service transferred me to three other people before I finally got on the line with someone who had some authority. His response was he'd send an email about who I should get in contact with."

"Figured as much." I shook my head.

"Is Colt sending someone out?" Steve asked.

"He's coming himself. He just got done out by Skip at the ME's office."

"And?" Steve asked.

"Waiting on the bullets to be removed so he can start on the ballistics reports. Nothing else to work with."

"Hello," a man called out. "Anyone in there?" His words were followed by the sound of knocking.

"Side door," Steve said.

We didn't get out of the living room before a man looking the better part of seventy entered the room. His face said that he was wondering who we were.

"Sir," I said.

"More friends of Ken's?" he asked. The guy looked

around the room at the torn-up and tossed-about furniture.

"Ken?" Steve asked.

"Ken Winter, the person who lives here."

"Are you a friend of his? A neighbor?" I asked.

"Ronald Spear. I live next door," he said. "Judging by the vehicle in the driveway, I'd say that you're the police again." He craned his neck, clearly trying to get a better look at the living room. "The gloves over the hands and destroyed house leave me a little concerned, though."

"I'm Lieutenant Nash Harrington. This is Sergeant Steve Walsh. Miami police."

"And where's Ken?" he asked.

"What do you mean *again*?" Steve asked. "You said *police again.*"

I was about to remind Steve that Tillerson had sent someone out when the neighbor continued. "There were police here with a search warrant yesterday, and now you," he said.

As far as I knew, no police were there with a warrant the day before. Tillerson mentioned having someone come out to the house, but they most certainly wouldn't have had a warrant, and that was just hours ago. "Can you tell us about the guys from yesterday?" I asked. "Did you talk to them?"

The scowl on the neighbor's face said he was troubled by something. "Can I see your badges?" he asked. "I think I should maybe call to check this all out. Something isn't right here."

Although the neighbor didn't have any say about our being in the house and had no right to ask us to explain ourselves, I wanted the guy's story and opted for the attract-more-flies-with-honey-than-vinegar approach. On top of that, the man was doing what any good neighbor would do, checking out something he felt was fishy next door. I figured the quicker we allowed him to vet us, the quicker we would get the guy's story on the so-called other officers. I showed him my badge, had him call our station, and told him to ask for Captain Halloway in the Homicide Bureau. The captain quickly told the guy who we were so we could proceed.

"Why is the Homicide Bureau sniffing around Ken's place. Where is he?" the neighbor, Ronald Spear, asked. "He's not…"

I didn't see any reason to keep Frost's cover or the fact that he'd been killed. "Ken, which wasn't his real name, was an undercover officer for the Miami PD. This morning, we found out that he was killed working a case," I said.

Mr. Spear grimaced. I imagined he wasn't expecting the news that, one, his neighbor wasn't who he thought he was and, two, had been killed.

"We're just getting going on this investigation. What can you tell us about the guys that showed up to this house with the warrant?" I asked.

"Geez, um…" He paused for a moment, as if in thought. "They drove a Camry," he said. "Maybe five years old. Gold. I thought it was an odd car for detectives. Thought maybe they were undercover or just driving one of their personal cars or something."

I pulled out my notepad and wrote the vehicle information down. "Didn't happen to get a license plate number, did you?"

"No," he said.

"How do you know they were detectives?" Steve asked.

"That's what the one guy said."

"So, you talked to them?" I asked.

"Just the one," he said. "And I wouldn't really say 'talked.' I was in my backyard and saw the two guys at the door of the garage. I kind of leaned over the fence and asked what was going on. The one guy said they were the police serving a search warrant. He asked me to go back inside my house."

"How many were there?" Steve asked.

"Two guys." Mr. Spear puffed his chest up. "Muscle Beach types. Both were well over six foot. Both were probably almost three hundred pounds."

The description matched that of the guys we saw on the boat footage. It also fit with the size of the shoe print pressed into the dirt a few feet away.

"Do you not know who they were?" he asked. "Were they not the police?"

"I can't say. As far as we know, no one from our department was out here, and there hasn't been any kind of search warrant issued that I know of."

"Dammit. I thought about calling the police too," Mr. Spear said. "Just to double-check."

"What can you tell us about the guys, aside from being big?" I asked. "Long hair, short hair, hair color? Any visible tattoos?"

"They were both bald. One of them had a dark-colored beard. The other, the guy who told me that they had a search warrant, was clean shaved. I didn't notice any tattoos."

"Do you have a guess at an age?" I asked.

"Thirties," Mr. Spear said. "Forty at the oldest."

"Did they leave with anything?" I asked.

"Not that I saw. I only saw them around the garage. They must have already been through the main house and guesthouse by the time I noticed them. I went over there after the guys left and closed all the doors that they left open. I mean, it looked like they broke the latches, but I don't know. It seemed the neighborly thing to do, I guess."

"What time do you think this was?" I asked. "That the men were here?"

"Had to be right around one in the afternoon. The one guy asked me to go in my house, and I did, for just a second. When I walked in, I remember hearing the opening theme song for one of my wife's soap operas. I did a one eighty and went right back outside. As I came back out, I saw the two guys walk from Ken's garage. Or whoever he was. The pair got in their car and left after that."

"Did the man that talked to you have any kind of an accent?" Steve asked.

"Accent? Like what kind?"

"Just anything distinctive," Steve said.

Mr. Spear shook his head. "No. Not that I picked up on."

"What can you tell us about your neighbor?" I asked. "Who you knew as Ken."

"Not a ton. He moved in maybe three or four months ago. Single guy. Said he'd come from Naples. He seemed like he was well off with the fancy Italian car, and he said he was in luxury real estate, which seemed like it fit with the expensive rental."

"Expensive rental?" Steve asked.

"The house is a rental."

"Oh," Steve said, nodding.

"Yeah, some developer owns it. Been that way for a couple years now. The old owner was named Jerry. He lived there maybe ten years. Financial guy that got a little too greedy and basically ripped a bunch of people off. Thankfully, not me. The house got seized, I think, and auctioned off. It had been empty for almost six months before Ken moved in. I think they wanted almost twelve grand a month on the lease."

I imagined that the lease was being covered by the department. I also imagined that it probably wasn't going over very well with the department's bean counters. Fancy cars were easy to come by and easy to loan out. Lodging, on the other hand, was not. Yet the easiest and safest thing for the undercover guys to do was rent a condo or house like any other person would. Vice would never risk their guy's cover by plunking them down in a department-owned home.

"Did you ever notice people coming and going from here?" I asked.

"I literally don't think that I've ever seen one person over here that didn't work for the landscaping company," Mr. Spear said.

Steve and I went through another handful of questions with the guy before thanking him for talking with us and sending him back to his place. We needed to get the house combed over and do whatever we could to find out who the hell these two mystery guys were.

CHAPTER 10

Manny

Manny turned from the mudroom into the kitchen. The faint smell of a cigar burning filled his airways. Frank sat on the kitchen's huge quartz-topped island and tapped away at the screen of his phone. He wore swim trunks and flip-flops, nothing else. A big, faded globe-and-eagle USMC tattoo took up a good portion of Frank's chest. Justin had the refrigerator door open and was blankly staring at the contents.

"What's up?" Frank asked. He took his eyes from his phone momentarily. "Are you working right now?" Frank motioned up and down and seemed to be referencing Manny's attire.

Manny glanced down at himself. He wore a light-blue button-down shirt, tan shorts, and sandals. He imagined the question was due to him wearing his gun in his shoulder holster in the house. "Yeah, on the clock."

"Looking for Matt?" Frank asked.

"Yeah," Manny said.

"He's in the living room."

Justin pulled a beer from the refrigerator and twisted off the top. "I'm heading out back," he said. "I need to skim the pool."

Frank grunted a response while staring down at his phone.

Manny started for the hallway.

"I have those girls coming back later," Frank said. "Tiffany was asking about you."

Manny stopped walking and turned toward Frank. "Asking what?"

"Just if you were going to be here. She said she thought you were hot. She liked that you spoke to her in Spanish."

"I don't put a lot of stock in what women who are being paid to be here say," Manny said. "I think feigning interest is part of the job."

"She's being paid to be here and drink and have a good time. Maybe paid a little extra for other things. Her asking about you is something else, though."

Manny shrugged.

"I think they're going to bring a couple more friends this time," Frank said. "Why don't you have some drinks with us later? Hang out for a bit?" Frank grabbed the bottle of beer beside him and took a big pull.

"Maybe," Manny said. "There are a couple things that I need to take care of first."

"Well, we'll be at the pool. The girls are paid for. May as well have some fun."

Manny nodded and again started walking to the hall that led across the house to the living room.

"You've got to enjoy the spoils while you can, Manny,"

Frank said. "You never know when this crazy ride may come to a sudden stop for you." Frank paused. "Or me, or anyone. You know?"

Manny glanced over his shoulder at Frank, nodded, and left the room, thinking that Frank's parting words were odd.

Manny walked the wide Spanish-tiled corridor to the living room a hundred feet ahead. To his right, framed art hung on the wall, broken up only by a bathroom and a pair of guest bedrooms. To his left was nothing but glass, floor to ceiling, that looked out at the front courtyard and detached eight-car garage. Next to the big fountain center in the courtyard, Paul and Eric stood outside of Eric's truck that they'd just arrived in. A beaten and bloodied Carlos Tavaras was lying in the back.

Manny entered through the open double doors of the living room and saw Matt slouched in a leather chaise. Matt stared up at the huge television bolted inside an alcove above the ten-foot-wide fireplace.

"Eric and Paul picked up—" Manny said. He cut his sentence short when he noticed Matt on the phone.

Matt held a big cigar in one hand, his phone to his ear in the other. He jammed the cigar in his mouth and held a finger up at Manny to give him a second.

"So, the place is set?" Matt asked. "Furniture, vehicles, food, electricity, television, internet."

Manny couldn't hear whoever was on the other end of the call answering the question.

"And we have everything necessary for two people?"

Again, a response apparently came.

"Good. Good. How are we on getting across the water?" Matt asked while he took a big pull from the cigar.

Manny watched as Matt blew a cloud of smoke into the air and waited on a response.

"Excellent," Matt said while nodding. "Friday morning."

Matt went quiet while listening to the person on the other end of the call. He chuckled at whatever was being said. "Perfect. Good work. I'll be in touch." Matt ended the call and set his phone on the arm of the chaise.

"Something up?" Manny asked.

Matt didn't respond. He reached out and placed his smoldering cigar into a big glass ashtray on the end table then scooped up a pen and a small notepad of paper. He jotted something down, tore the page off, and jammed the paper into the pocket of his shorts. He tossed the notepad on the table. Matt rubbed at his nose with the back of his hand. "As soon as everything is in place, I'll need you to pack for a few days."

"For?"

"You and I are going to take a little trip," Matt said. "Expansion with our neighbors to the south. I was just chatting with a contact of mine down there. He's putting some things together for us."

"All right," Manny said. He furrowed his brow. Matt's entire operation began in Miami and spread to the north, east, and west. As far as Manny's memory served, Matt had never once mentioned knowing anyone south. He wanted a clarification. "Are we talking Cuba, South America, what?"

"Once everything is hashed out, we'll get into all the

details," Matt said. He scooped up his cigar from the ashtray and put it in his mouth. Matt squinted from the smoke rising into his right eye. "What were you saying when you walked in?"

"Paul and Eric found Tavaras. They just pulled up out front with him."

Matt didn't immediately respond. He appeared to be in thought. "Paul is here now?"

"And Eric, yeah."

"Okay. Have them take Tavaras down to the shed by the water. Put the tarp down so the cleanup is easier."

"It's going like that?"

"Yeah," Matt said.

"I'll go and tell them." Manny turned to leave the living room.

"Call them," Matt said.

"They're right out front."

"I know. Just call them and have them put him in the shed. You and I need to talk about something quick."

"Um, okay," Manny said. He dialed Paul, who answered within a few rings.

"Yeah," Paul said.

"Matt wants Tavaras taken to the shed by the boathouse. Put the tarp down."

"And then?" Paul asked.

"Hold on." Manny took the phone from his mouth. "You want them to just tie him up or something?"

"I don't give a shit. Tie him, strap him, chain him, rope him. Just make sure he's in the shed and the tarp is down.

They can make him a damn drink and put a movie on for him for all I care. Just get Tavaras in the shed and wait until we get down there," Matt said.

"Just take him to the shed and wait for us," Manny said into the phone.

"Sure," Paul said.

Manny clicked off from the call. "Taken care of. Now what's up? What did you want to talk about?"

"Grab a seat." Matt motioned to the couch.

Manny walked over and plopped down. While a normal chat with Matt was nothing to be concerned about, Manny had a growing feeling that something was off, that something was wrong.

"I need you to do something," Matt said. "A couple of things, actually. You probably aren't going to like it, but it's necessary."

"Sure. What?"

"After we're done with Tavaras, after we get answered what we need answered, I need you to put Paul down."

"What?" Manny asked. "For what?"

"After we got back from the store, I got a phone call. The cops have Paul's name in connection with Frost and Nance."

Manny shook his head, not quite believing what he was hearing. "What? How?"

"I don't know. But they have it. You guys had gloves on, right? Never touched the bodies without gloves? Never touched anything in connection to Frost or Nance or the dock at that house?"

"Matt, I never saw Paul or Eric touch anything. I mean,

73

we were gloved up when we were loading Frost and Nance into the boat, gloved up when we took the boat to the house, and gloved up when they were left on that dock."

"Has he been talking to anyone about Frost and Nance? Maybe asking questions on the streets about the two?"

"I mean, we were asking around a little before we knew they were cops," Manny said.

"Maybe it had something to do with that. There had to have been a slipup somewhere. I don't know. I don't know the specifics on how they got it. All I know is that his name is going around the Miami Police Department. Shit, who knows, maybe he was working with the two of them."

"He wasn't working with the cops."

"Do you know that for certain?" Matt asked. "Would you bet your life on it?"

Manny let out a big puff of air. "I don't know. No."

"Exactly. Honestly, it no longer matters at this point how they got his name. They have it. He needs to go."

"Son of a bitch," Manny said. "You're sure on this? This can't be avoided? I mean, even if he did get pinched, he isn't going to talk."

"That's a chance that we won't be taking," Matt said.

CHAPTER 11

The last few hours of my workday passed in a blur. Colt had met us at the house that Frost had been staying in. He printed the entire place from top to bottom. From there, Colt accompanied us to the home that Nance had been leasing under the guise of being Aaron Kraft. The home was a remodeled ranch on a canal that led out to the bay. Like the home that Frost had leased, the place had been broken into and ransacked. We spoke with several neighbors, but no one had mentioned seeing whoever had gone into the home. Colt took prints from the place and returned to the station. Just before I left the office for the night, he called me with an update. The shoe print appeared to be a size sixteen, and not one of the prints he took returned a hit that didn't belong to either Frost or Nance.

I pulled the Bronco into my driveway right around seven forty-five. My father's truck, a two-year-old black Ford F-150, was nowhere to be seen—my parents must have run out for something. The garage door was open, and Amy's car sat inside. I parked the Bronco and pulled the handle for the door—it didn't open. I mumbled under my breath and reached my hand out of the open window to pull the exterior door handle to let myself out. The interior handle had been acting up for probably a week. I stepped out and swung the door closed. It rattled, clanked and dropped some rust flakes on my driveway. The Bronco had been losing its battle with time for quite a while. As much as I had a soft spot for her, the reality was she wasn't going to last much longer in her current state. With the truck having too much sentimental value to scrap, I'd been toying with the idea of a full restoration.

I didn't get two steps toward my front door when my phone rang. I yanked it from my pocket, and Tillerson's name was on the screen. I swiped Talk and brought the phone to my ear. "Hello."

"Hey, it's Tillerson. I think I have a name," he said. "And it looks promising."

"What's the name, and how did we get it?"

"The name is Paul Lattore. Big ol' guy. Six six and two eighty. Address in South Miami. The guy has a hell of a spotty past. Assault after assault charge. A couple of small stretches of time spent inside. All the charges and time spent was from out of state, though. I got the word from a CI that this Lattore had been asking questions on the streets about some real estate guys that were distributing."

"That size and weight match up with everything that we have."

"I know. I've been looking into the guy to see who he runs with. Asking my people. Seems no one has really heard of him other than the one CI. I tried reaching out to Mullin with the name, to see if he knew of the guy. Haven't heard back from him yet."

"Let's get this Lattore picked up," I said. I put my foot up onto the truck's front bumper, which moved more than it probably should have. I took my foot from it and opted to lean against it instead.

"I already contacted the locals and asked them to make a little house call for us," Tillerson said. "Aside from that, I have every person at my disposal on the streets and on patrol looking for Lattore. As soon as I hear anything back, I'll forward that information on to you."

"Perfect," I said. "Are you working all night, or what?"

"I'll be here for another few hours, but I'm going to have to try to sleep sometime."

"Have you talked to Dave?"

"Yeah, a little bit ago. He gave me a rundown of what you guys found."

"I wish we had more, but Wade couldn't do a ton with the video footage that we picked up. He said it seemed like they were wearing buffs over their faces, so even if he could get a good close-up, we probably wouldn't get anything to work with."

"I talked to him," Tillerson said. "He told me the same. Said that maybe the guy piloting the boat had longer hair that was hanging down out of the back of his hat."

"I didn't get that part," I said.

"He wasn't certain, just said it kind of looked like it. Like maybe he had braids or dreads."

"Okay. We'll see if it leads to anything. What's going on with getting ahold of Nance's family?" I asked.

"I tried the contact we had for his mother, but it's some kind of assisted living facility. I asked to be put through to her room, but the woman that I spoke with, a nurse, mentioned advanced Alzheimer's. She gave me contact information for Nance's brother. I left him a message, looking for a callback. I haven't heard anything yet, though."

"All right. Pass whatever you get to Dave and the night shift guys but keep me in the loop."

"You got it," Tillerson said.

"I'll talk to you in the morning, if not sooner." I ended the call and headed to my front door. It opened before I could get to it. Lucky shot out in a tan streak and mauled me like she normally did. She hopped and squealed. Licked and whined like she hadn't seen me in weeks. I gave her a petting and sent her back toward the door.

Lucky passed Amy, who stood in the doorway. "Heard your truck," Amy said. She pulled her dark hair back and used a tie that had been around her wrist to put it into a ponytail. "Then you didn't come in, so we were just investigating."

"I got a call."

"Work?" she asked.

"Yeah. Seems like we got a little bit of a lead."

"Good," she said. Amy put her arms around my neck and gave me a kiss. "I can't imagine what these guys' families are going through." She shook her head.

"We'll find whoever is responsible," I said.

"I know," she said.

I'd talked to Amy a few times throughout the day and given her a vague overview of the investigation—basically that a pair of undercover officers had been murdered while working a case. She didn't care for the details.

"How are people at the office?" she asked.

"Not a lot of people in our department knew them—which kind of comes with working undercover in Vice. I'd only seen the one of them a handful of times, the other just once. Either way, they were some of our own. We all feel it. Everyone is going to do every damn thing that they can to find out who is behind it."

Amy nodded.

I let out a big breath. I needed to shut the case off in my head or it would take over the rest of my night. I wanted my parents to enjoy the time that they spent with us, and Amy had seen me stew on cases more times than I could count. "Enough with work," I said. "What's the plan? Where did my parents go?"

"They ran to the store," Amy said.

I motioned past her into the house, and we walked inside.

"My mom went to get her stuff to make snickerdoodles?" I asked.

"No. She already did that." Amy pointed toward the kitchen. "She even bought little tins to put them in."

"Cool," I said. I went to the kitchen, took off my suit jacket, which I tossed over a kitchen chair, and went for the cookies. "So where did they go?" I popped the top off a tin and snatched a cookie from inside.

"Your dad wanted to grill out. Your mom said something about making homemade potato salad. They went to go buy everything."

I nodded, took a bite of cookie, and jammed the rest of it in my mouth. I went for another. "Did you have any of these?" I asked, talking around a mouthful.

"There were three tins earlier. Your dad and I dusted one already."

"Yeah, she can bake the hell out of some snickerdoodles," I said. "Out of anything, really. When I was a kid, she used to make these homemade doughnuts." I shook my head. "Damn. That and she had a thing for making me grilled cheeses and milkshakes. Hell, she did that into my thirties. Every time I went to their house, bam, grilled cheese and a milkshake."

"How are you not, like, five hundred pounds?" Amy asked. "I've seriously gained five pounds since they've been here."

"Fighting crime burns a lot of calories," I said. I scooped another cookie from the tin.

CHAPTER 12

Manny

Manny walked to the service door of the white stucco shed with the tile roof. The building, about the size of a two-car garage, contained all the pool equipment and gear for the grounds crew. The roll-up door on the leftmost side was closed, and Manny couldn't see inside through the shuttered windows that faced the house. He banged on the service door, which pulled open a moment later. Paul held the door and stepped to the side so Manny could enter.

Smack in the middle of the room was a blue tarp, and bound to a chair sitting in the center of it was a small Hispanic male—Tavaras. A few lawnmowers were parked on the left-hand side of the room, and some rakes and shovels hung from hooks on the walls. The back wall of the room had a big washbasin, which came in handy when cleaning up the blood after Matt shot Frost and Nance. The right side of the room had coiled hoses, ropes, straps, and some five-gallon pails filled with cement.

Manny had eyes locked on Tavaras. He looked to be in

rough shape. Both eyes were swollen. A big cut hung open above his right eye. Tavaras's chin was pressed against the chest of his blood-soaked green T-shirt. His jeans were bloodied, torn, and dirt covered. "What's he saying?" Manny asked.

"Not a lot through a broken jaw," Eric said.

"Who broke his jaw?" Manny asked.

"It may have been me," Paul said. "I don't know. He was running his mouth, so I popped him in it, and his chin went a little sideways. He can still talk. He's fine."

"You said soften him up," Eric said. "He's soft."

"It looks like it," Manny said.

"Is the boss coming?" Eric asked.

"He's on his way down from the house," Manny said.

"Please," Tavaras mumbled, "I didn't know they were cops."

Manny stared at him and watched blood roll down his chin as he muttered the single sentence.

"You came to me asking if I could set a meeting between Matt and two guys who ended up being cops. If we had taken that meeting, based on your judgment and vetting, we would have all been done. Our whole business gone."

"I didn't tell them anything," Tavaras said.

"How did they know about the carpet-cleaning businesses?" Manny asked.

Tavaras didn't respond.

Manny put eyes on Eric. "Where did you pick him up?"

"From his condo in North Miami," Eric said. "I bet we went past his three properties ten times each before this jerk ever showed up."

"Where's his vehicle?" Manny asked.

"Still in the garage there," Paul said.

"Did anyone see you?"

"It was the middle of the day," Paul said. "There were people all over."

Manny gave him a look, questioning just what the hell he was talking about.

Paul continued. "We knocked on his door. I told him that someone would like a word with him. Told him that it was in his best interest financially and otherwise to come to a meeting."

"And he just came along?" Manny asked.

"No. He asked what we wanted, to which I simply said that I wasn't going to ask him to come along twice," Paul said.

"And then he pulled a gun," Eric said.

"Yeah. The prick yanks a pistol from his waistline, so I gave him a little tap on the cheek and then disarmed him. We entered his place, and I continued to rough him up to make him more compliant. Eric dealt with the woman and other man inside the property."

"Woman and man?" Manny asked.

"Yeah. Some guy with braids and some skank that were sitting on his couch," Paul said. "They looked like users."

"How were they dealt with?" Manny asked.

"Permanently," Paul said.

"You shot them?" Manny's eyes went to Eric.

"No. Too many people around for that," Eric said. "Someone would have heard the shots. I snapped the woman's neck and crushed the guy's head on the corner of the kitchen island. Sank his skull in."

"You left the bodies there?" Manny asked.

"Well, yeah, what the hell were we supposed to do with them?" Eric asked.

"There was only one suitcase, and this little shit here was the only one small enough to fit," Paul added. He nodded at Tavaras.

"Suitcase?" Manny asked.

"We had to get him from his condo to the truck somehow," Paul said.

Manny rubbed his eyes. "How does picking up a hundred-pound little piece of shit turn into two other people killed and you two idiots jamming a guy in a suitcase?"

"We had to improvise. He's here, isn't he?" Paul said.

"So, when someone notices the stink, and the police show up to find two bodies, and those same police start digging around for security footage, then what?"

"I didn't see any cameras anywhere," Paul said.

"Yeah, we parked a block over," Eric said.

"You took your truck?" Manny asked.

"Yeah." Eric nodded. "Why?"

"Did you pull your plates?"

"We parked a block over," Eric said.

A bang came on the door. Paul went to answer it.

Matt walked in, gave the guys a quick glance, and went straight for Tavaras. He crouched in front of him. "I want the whole story about you and the cops that were posing as real estate developers. The cops who you tried setting me up with. If you give me an ounce of bullshit, I'll send my guys out to visit your mother. Your sister if you have one. Aunties and nieces. Your granny if she's still alive. They'll all be brought here and killed in front of you."

Tavaras mumbled something that Manny couldn't make out. More blood ran from his mouth.

Matt looked over his shoulder. "What's wrong with his mouth?"

"His jaw is broken," Manny said.

Matt turned toward Tavaras and grabbed him by the chin. He shoved his head back. "Are you going to answer my questions?"

Tavaras screamed. "Yes!"

"Good." Matt took his hand from his face. "The cops. Start to finish."

Manny leaned against the roll-up garage door and watched as the guy mumbled his story. Tavaras said that through a couple of men who worked for him, he and Frost arranged a meeting. When he met with Frost, Frost said he was looking to expand his transportation business. Tavaras claimed that the distribution was currently being handled by a carpet-cleaning business and wasn't sure if they were looking to expand. Tavaras said he told the undercovers that it wasn't his call, but for a percentage, he could try to get them a meeting with someone who could make that decision. It was then that he contacted Manny. Tavaras claimed that was the entire story. He didn't waver from the story an inch as Matt used garden shears to remove a finger. He didn't reveal who told him about the carpet cleaning business with the removal of a little toe.

"Paul," Matt said. "Come here."

Paul stepped onto the tarp and walked over. He stopped a few inches short of the growing blood pool forming beneath Tavaras's chair. "Kill him."

Paul removed his weapon from a shoulder holster and pointed it at Tavaras. Tavaras looked up at Paul.

"Head or chest?" Paul asked.

"Just get it over with," Matt said.

From only a few inches away, Paul took aim on Tavaras's forehead and squeezed the trigger.

Matt looked at Manny and gave him a nod.

Manny left the door he leaned against and headed to Paul, who was staring down at Tavaras, who'd slumped over in his chair. Manny pulled his weapon and lifted it to Paul's back.

"What the hell," Eric said.

Paul turned around, and Manny fired twice. Both rounds entered Paul's chest. He stumbled backward and fell, knocking the chair-bound Tavaras to the ground. Manny took another two steps to Paul, who lay on the tarp. Paul touched the entry wounds on his chest and looked at his hand. Manny fired a single round into the side of Paul's forehead, and Paul went flat on the tarp—still.

"What the hell is going on?" Eric's voice was loud, frantic.

"The cops had his name," Matt said. "We got word earlier."

"Had his name for what?" Eric asked.

"In connection to Frost. This was the only way," Matt said. "Let's get this cleaned up."

"What do you want done with the bodies?" Manny asked. He crouched at Tavaras and began to work the rope that was binding him. "We haven't got another boat yet."

"Where is Paul's Lexus?" Matt asked.

"Off to the side of the garages," Manny said.

"Stick them in the trunk of Paul's car and wait. I have to arrange something."

"I don't know if that trunk is going to be big enough," Manny said. "Damn, who the hell tied this?"

"These two combined make two normal-sized guys," Matt said. He pointed at the two bodies on the ground, Paul's large one and Tavaras's small.

Manny gave Matt a quick glance and shifted his attention to Eric. "Come here," Manny said. "Help me get this dude untied from his chair."

Eric's face scrunched. He shook his head. "Paul would have never said anything. No matter what. He wasn't a snitch."

"That wasn't a chance we could take. Now, come on," Manny said.

"This is messed up, man. How the hell would the cops have had his name?" Eric asked.

"Would you get your ass over here and help me with these two?"

Eric again shook his head. He stared at Paul's body and reluctantly stepped forward onto the tarp.

Manny rose from his spot beside Tavaras. "See if you can get this rope free," he said. "I can't get the damn thing."

Eric crouched and reached for the rope. Manny put the gun to the back of Eric's head and pulled the trigger. Blood spattered across the bodies of Tavaras and Paul. Eric fell flat across the top of the two.

"What was that about?" Matt asked.

"These two idiots took Eric's truck to pick up Tavaras in broad daylight. Didn't cover the plates and left two bodies in Tavaras's condo. It would just be a matter of time before the cops were on to him, and we would have had to do it then." Manny holstered his gun and snapped the thumb break. "May as well just get the shit out of the way now."

Matt shrugged.

"This is kind of what I meant when I said we won't be able to fit everyone in the trunk," Manny said. "But it's fine. I'll toss Eric in the back of his truck and go dump it somewhere as soon as I'm done with Tavares and Paul."

"I have something that I want done with them," Matt said. "Grab Justin and have him help you get them loaded."

"Okay," Manny said. "You want me to sniff around and see if Tavaras told any of his guys anything?"

"If anyone knows anything and then hears what happened to their boss, they ain't talking."

"Well, if you want me to, let me know."

"All right. I need to make a couple phone calls. If you see Frank up at the house, tell him I don't want any women coming onto the property until this is all cleaned up."

"I'll let him know."

"Good work, Manny," Matt said. "I know that wasn't the easiest thing to do. You did well."

Manny nodded and walked from the shed.

CHAPTER 13

I'd gotten only one update as the night went on. Tillerson called saying he was shutting it down for the evening. His call came a few minutes after eleven o'clock. Tillerson said the address we had on Paul Lattore, a condo, turned out to be a bust. The people who currently resided there didn't know of a forwarding address. Tillerson had put out a BOLO for Lattore's vehicle, a Lexus sedan that was a few years old.

I woke up, alone in bed, shortly after seven in the morning. There was no Amy, no Lucky. I didn't hear anyone talking. After a brief shower and shave, I got dressed and left my bedroom. As I walked the hall, the smells of something cooking filled my nose. I wandered out to the kitchen to see my mother, short and mostly gray-haired, standing in front of the stove. Lucky had taken a position at my mother's ankle and gave me a dismissive glance and went back to staring up at my mother, who I was certain was feeding her a good portion of whatever she was cooking. I looked out my patio doors. My father and Amy sat at our patio table. Amy must have seen me looking out. She smiled and waved.

"Morning, hon," my mom said as she glanced over at me. "Coffee is ready. It just beeped."

I went to the coffeepot, grabbed a cup from the cupboard, and filled it.

"What time do you have to go in?" my mother asked.

"I'll probably head out in about a half hour."

"Okay. Well, breakfast is just about ready. Go sit with your dad and Amy. I'll bring everything out in a second."

I took a sip of my coffee and leaned against the counter. "What did you make?"

"Biscuits and gravy." She stuck a spoon into the pan on the stove and gave it a taste. "Gravy that needs more pepper." She tossed the spoon into the sink.

I walked over and got a look at the gravy as my mother added more pepper. Two pies sitting on the counter caught my eye. "What are these?"

"Those are for later," she said. "I made them this morning."

"What the hell time did you get up?"

"Mouth!" she scolded.

"What? I asked what time you got up."

"You said hell."

"And?"

"Just leave the sailor talk at work." She shook her head. "I've been up since around five."

"Five? What the hell did you get up at five for?"

"Nash Douglas!" She snapped her head toward me. "One more time and you're going to get it."

I looked down at her and smiled. My eyes went back to the pies on the counter. One looked to be cherry, the other apple. The apple one had a small piece missing. I put my finger to some of the filling for a little taste.

"Hey!" my mother shouted. She swatted my hand. "Get your finger out of there. I said those are for later. Why are you in my kitchen?"

"My kitchen," I said. "And there's already a piece missing."

"That was your father. And he got swatted a lot harder than you did. Now go." She jerked her head at the patio doors.

I smiled and went outside.

My father had his back to me. Even at almost seventy, he was still pretty wide-shouldered. He wore a red flannel shirt, sweatpants, and slippers—old-guy morning attire dialed to perfection. He looked over his shoulder at me. His gray-and-white hair was a couple of inches long and mussed from being fresh out of bed. I doubted he felt the need to take a comb to it—I imagined it would remain that way the rest of the day. He and Amy sounded like they were in midconversation. That conversation stopped dead the second I arrived. They both looked at me—and said nothing.

"Interrupting something?" I asked.

"No," my father said.

"Nope." Amy shook her head.

Both answers sounded like lies.

"Right," I said. I walked to the table, set my cup of coffee down, and had a seat. "It's pretty early for bullshit. So, what were you two just talking about?"

"Aside from your mother, this here is about the most

beautiful girl I've ever seen. She's got a good heart. A good compass. Maybe you should get married and have some grandkids for your mother and me to spoil before we die."

My father wasn't one for beating around the bush. I shouldn't have pressed for an answer on what they were talking about. It was too early to come up with a well-thought-out response. "Is that what you two were out here discussing?" I asked. The question was more a stalling tactic, as I was pretty certain they were discussing that and even surer that they wouldn't admit it.

Neither responded, as I figured. The silence began to grow awkward, as if I was supposed to say something further on the topic. The patio door slid open, and my mother came out with two big bowls, saving me from having to come up with something to say. One bowl was filled with biscuits, fresh from the oven. The other bowl had the gravy. I piled up a plate.

Just as I brought the last forkful of breakfast to my mouth, my phone rang—Dave.

I swiped the screen of my phone to answer the call. "Yeah, Dave," I said and scooted away from the patio table. I went to the house and entered through the sliding patio door.

"We have Frost's and Nance's cars."

"Where at?"

"Both are in the driveway of a waterfront home just south of the John F. Kennedy Causeway on the upper east side."

"Both at the same spot?" I asked.

"Yeah."

"How did we find them?"

"A Realtor showed up at the house. He was there to meet some people that were going to drop off furniture to be staged or something. Anyway, he gets there, and the gate is standing open, and there's a pair of cars in the driveway. The place was supposed to be vacant. The listing agent called the police, the home was cleared, and the tags were run on the cars parked there. We got the call shortly after."

"Okay. Was there anything to suggest anyone was in the house at all? Forced entry or anything?"

"Nothing reported."

"All right." I checked the time on my phone—a quarter to eight. Dave's shift was ending, and the shifts for me and my guys were about to start.

"What do we have going on out there right now?" I asked.

"Local PD on the scene. Waiting on word of what to do."

"Damn. We're going to need Forensics to go through the cars. We'll need to get into the house. I'm going to have to make some calls."

"All right. Do you need me and my guys out there? We can lead things and pass it off to you daylighters as soon as you're all on scene."

"Nah, we'll get it, Dave. You guys already put in your shift. Why don't you text me the address, and I'll get over there. I'll make my calls as I drive."

"Are you sure?"

"Yeah. Have you seen Halloway yet this morning?"

"He just walked in a couple minutes ago," Dave said.

"All right. I'm just stopping in at the office to get a car and then heading straight out to the scene. I'll call him."

"Okay. You should see that text with the address as soon as I hang up."

"Thanks, Dave," I said.

I ended the call and dialed Halloway's desk as I filled a travel mug with coffee.

"Halloway," he answered.

"Cap, it's Harrington. Dave just called me. Looks like we got a location on the BOLO cars that Frost and Nance had. I'm going to stop at the office to get a cruiser and head straight out to where they were found."

"Where were they?" Halloway asked.

"I guess a vacant house for sale." I took the phone from my ear and looked at the screen. I rattled the address off to the captain as I popped a lid on my to-go cup.

"Was the place cleared?" the captain asked.

"It was."

"Okay. What do you need from me?" the captain asked.

"Let Forensics know that we're going to need them on location. We may end up needing a search warrant for the property. I'm not certain."

"I'll take care of it," Halloway said. "Are you going to have the team meet you out there?"

"I'm going to let Steve know what's up and play it by ear. Stop out there and see what we have. If I need them on scene, I'll call them out."

"All right. Give me an update when you have one."

"Will do, Cap." I ended the call, sent a text to Tillerson that the BOLO vehicles had been found, went to say my goodbyes, and scooped up my truck keys from the counter.

CHAPTER 14

Two police cruisers were parked in front of a barricade at the end of the street. As I slowed to pull to the side of the road, I could see the back of a black BMW sedan parked at the gated entrance. I couldn't see a house through the landscaping as I pulled to a stop behind the patrol cars. I killed the engine and stepped out. As I walked to the driveway and the open front gate, the big metal-roofed house hiding behind the lush landscaping and horizontal metal bars of the gate came into view. A pair of uniformed officers and a man dressed in a suit stood at the back of a Mercedes sedan in the driveway. In front of the Mercedes was a Porsche SUV. One of the officers, noticing me walking up, left the others and came down the driveway.

"Lieutenant Harrington, Homicide," I said as he approached. "Looks like you found our BOLO cars."

"Appears so," the officer said.

I put eyes on the open gate as I went past it. The metal bars looked bent.

"Someone stick a car through this gate?" I asked.

"Looks like they pushed it open, yeah," he said. "Officer

Larry Dillon. North District." Dillon's waistline strained the buttons on his dark-blue uniform. His cheeks were round, and his blond hair was buzzed short.

"Good to meet you." I shook his hand. "Is this the listing agent who called it in?" I asked, pointing my chin at the man in the suit standing with the other officer.

"Yeah. A company was coming to stage furniture, so the Realtor came out. He sees the open gate and the cars parked in the driveway. He immediately called us. There were no showings scheduled. The place wasn't even ready to be shown, he said. Officer Steinbrenner there was the first to arrive, and I was on scene a few minutes after."

It was pretty much the same story that Dave had given me. "No one in the house?" I asked.

"No. The Realtor let us inside, and we walked through the property. No signs that it had been entered or disturbed. The company that listed the house had cameras installed while the home was for sale. He said he'd show whatever it caught to anyone who needed to see it."

"Why would they have cameras installed?" I asked.

"Couldn't tell you," Dillon said. "We didn't get into that with him."

"All right. Let's check out the cars and have a chat with the listing agent," I said.

Dillon led me up the driveway to the two men. The other officer, Steinbrenner, looked to be in his mid-thirties. Black sunglasses rested on his short black hair. A small goatee wrapped his mouth. The listing agent was dressed in a designer suit. His hair was styled to perfection, and his shoes reflected sunlight. The guy was tall, maybe six foot four with a square chin and noticeably white veneers. Both officers and the real estate agent stood and watched as I did laps around the BOLO vehicles.

The cars were parked single file in front of the home's big wooden garage door. The second car in line, farthest from the house, was a big black Mercedes S-Class sedan, a car that Frost had been using. A dark-blue Porsche SUV, Nance's, was parked a couple of feet in front of it, closer to the garage. Both vehicles looked undisturbed. I tucked my hand into the sleeve of my suit jacket and, through it, tried a door on each vehicle—both locked. Whether Frost and Nance had driven the vehicles to the house or they'd simply been left there by someone else, I didn't know.

I looked up at the house. The big white two-story home had stack-stone trim and horizontal bars serving as a railing on a balcony. More of the horizontal bars served as a railing up to the elevated front door. Palm trees and plants and professional landscaping engulfed the home.

"In the market?" the agent asked.

"Maybe if I won the lottery," I said. "What's a place like this go for?"

"The listing price is an even three million, but the sellers are motivated," he said. "I think two point seven five would buy it."

"Yeah, different world than what I live in," I said. "What was the reason for installing cameras?"

"This was a vacation home of the owners. They've since purchased up the coast and moved just about everything from here to their new place near Harbor Beach in Fort Lauderdale. Yet some items remained here and were included with the purchase price of the home—some furniture, televisions, all the equipment in the home theater room, to name a few things. The appliances go with the property as well, all of which are top-of-the-line. With a home like this, sometimes it can take a few months to sell, and being vacant, the properties can become targets for thieves. When people list with our company, Luxe and Associates, we don't take any chances. The cost to us for the customer's peace of mind, as well as insuring the security of the home, is inconsequential."

"Mmm-hmm," I said. His last few sentences sounded like they were read straight from the mission statement of the real estate agency.

"We got someone here," Steinbrenner said. "One of yours?"

I looked down the driveway and saw someone with a big gray box staring at the open gate door—Colt. I'd called him on my drive, and he'd said that Halloway had given him the address.

"That's my forensics guy," I said.

Colt walked to us, introduced himself to the officers, and immediately got started on the vehicles. At my request, Dillon and Steinbrenner agreed to do some door knocking at the neighboring homes. The real estate agent, who told me his name was Rex Macdonald, took me through the home. He said that everything inside the place looked the same as he last saw it. Nothing appeared off. The alarm on the property would have triggered if someone had entered, and they had no indication that it did. The only thing damaged was the front gate, and if it hadn't been for the gate and the cars, there would have been no sign that anyone had even been there. As soon as we finished the walk-through inside, Macdonald led me out to the back.

The property's backyard, which had terraced decks, faced an inlet off the bay. Directly across the water was Belle Mead Island—an L-shaped island that held about fifty homes and was connected to land by a single bridge. I went past the rectangular pool and stepped down from one deck to the next. Areas of the deck had been built around towering palm trees—a pair that were roughly ten feet apart held a hammock. At the end of the deck, two gravel paths led toward the water. The path on the right led to a small gazebo and outdoor kitchen. I quickly had a look then went back to the other path, which led toward the dock. Aside from the water of the bay off to my left, the island before me, and the canal continuing past the property, there wasn't a ton to see—no boats tied up, nothing lying about, no blood.

"What do we have to do about seeing what these cameras caught?" I asked. "Did you need to call to get an okay or something?"

"That would be me who gives the okays. I own the agency."

"Apologies," I said. "I must have missed that."

"None needed. I just need to call the office and get some log-in information from my secretary. As soon as I have that, I can get connected to the home's internet, and we should be good," Macdonald said. "The video is cloud-based and stores for a week. I was here last Wednesday, and these cars weren't here, so these cars getting here should be on there."

"All right. Let's see what, if anything, we've got."

Macdonald led the way, and I followed him to the front of the property.

"Let me just go to the car, make this call, and then get signed on. I'll be right back," he said.

"Sure," I said.

I went to Colt as Macdonald walked to his car.

"Anything?" I asked.

"Locked up tight," Colt said. He adjusted his navy-blue forensics hat that matched his T-shirt. "I took some prints from a few spots on the cars, but I'm not really seeing a ton to work with on the exterior. Maybe we'll have better luck inside. I'm going to have to get the cars towed back to the garages at the office and get into them. Keys would help," he said. Colt had a print in hand that he'd just pulled off the Mercedes trunk lid. He pressed the tape he held to a backing and placed it inside his open kit a few feet away.

"I imagine they would, but I haven't seen any keys here. I can't remember seeing keys at either of the homes that these two were staying at. Maybe try calling Impound, which is where I assume the cars originally came from. Or the dealerships."

"I'll figure it out," Colt said. He flipped the top of his kit closed and stretched his back as he stood up straight. "Did you see anything inside or out back that I should have a closer look at?"

"I didn't see anything in the house. The North District officers said they went through the place and didn't see anything either. The same goes for out back. These may have just been parked here," I said. I held out two fingers at the pair of vehicles. "That front gate may be worth checking out."

"Okay. I'll try to lift some prints from the home's doors as well. You never know. You said that we had some video?" Colt asked.

"This Macdonald guy owns the company the home is listed through. He's getting some log-in information from his office, and we should be good to go." I looked down the driveway, and Macdonald was walking toward Colt and me. "Here he comes now."

"We're set," Macdonald said. "Do you have a day and time that you're looking for?"

"No. We just need to see when these vehicles got here," I said.

"All right. This tablet is kind of small and hard to see in the sun," Macdonald said. "Did you want to just head inside? I think I can screen cast this to one of the televisions in there."

"That's fine," I said.

"I'm going to check out that front gate, and then I'll meet you guys inside," Colt said. "Get a look at whatever the cameras caught and see if there are some other places that I need to go over." He walked to his kit and scooped it up.

CHAPTER 15

Macdonald had just rewound the footage after we saw the cars moving on screen.

"What's that time say?" I asked. I squinted and looked at the time stamp in the top right corner of the television bolted to the wall in the kitchen.

"A couple minutes after eleven o'clock," Macdonald said. "This is from Monday night."

The camera feed that we watched was from the front gate—which was already open. We would have to go back further to see who had opened the gate—and how.

The Porsche SUV being driven by Nance, we assumed, pulled through the open gate. Following the SUV was the black Mercedes sedan—Frost. Again, an assumption.

The two vehicles pulled up the driveway single file and left the camera's view.

"Do we have another view that catches the driveway itself?" I asked.

"Yeah, one second. I think the front door one should be what we're looking for." Macdonald tapped away at the screen of the tablet he held and brought up the other view.

While the angle of the camera was meant to catch anyone standing on the front stoop, the driveway and vehicles were clearly visible. We watched as someone exited the Mercedes and met whoever left the Porsche. The pair stood there and talked at the back of the SUV. No way could I make a positive identification that either of the people on the screen were Frost or Nance, yet the body proportions seemed about right.

"How are we looking?" Colt asked.

I pointed at the television on the wall. "Two people driving our BOLO vehicles pulled into the driveway and got out of the cars."

Colt took up a spot beside me and set his kit at his feet. "Frost and Nance?"

"You tell me," I said.

"Yeah, too dark and far away from the camera to make an ID," Colt said.

On screen, the pair lit up momentarily. The source of light seemed to be the screen of a cell phone held by the man we believed was Frost.

"Looks like they have cell phones," Colt said. "We didn't find any anywhere, did we?"

"No," I said. "And Tillerson said that the guys only used burners while undercover. No way to track them, and getting the tower information would only give us a rough triangulation—that's if we could get it from whatever phone company the burner phones piggybacked from. Same goes for call history."

"Makes sense," Colt said. "These two were posing as

criminals. What criminal is going to give the law a way to find them and who they've been talking to?"

"I get the logic behind it," I said.

"Speaking of Tillerson, was he coming out here?"

"Yeah. Though he should have probably been here by now. I'll call and see what his status is in a second. Did we get anything from the front gate?"

"I lifted some paint," Colt said. "Metallic silver."

"Good," I said. "We haven't gotten that deep into the video to see what pushed it in yet, but hopefully we can match it up."

From the corner of my eye, I saw Colt nod beside me. On screen, the pair looked to be leaving the driveway and walking through the side yard to the back of the property.

"So, they pulled up, waited out front for a few minutes, and then went out back?" Colt asked. "When was this video taken?"

"Around eleven at night, Monday," I said. "A little after. And that's about the extent of what they did so far. Maybe they got a message. Could have been that phone lighting up."

"Logical," Colt said.

"Do we have any cameras that cover the rear of this place?" I asked.

"Just ones that cover the pool area and patio doors that lead into the house," Macdonald said.

"Let's pull that up," I said.

"Hold on." Macdonald again switched the camera view, and the backyard pool area popped up on screen. We saw the pair walk through the frame, across the deck, and toward the water. They disappeared from view, yet the short time they were in it, we had a better look at them.

"Nothing that catches the water?" I asked.

"Sorry," Macdonald said. "This is it as far as the back of the grounds."

I made a note of the time that they walked through the frame—eleven fourteen and some change. "Fast-forward and see if they ever come back," I said.

Macdonald sped up the footage to ten times the usual speed, and we let it play. Twenty minutes passed, over three hours of real-time footage, without them ever coming back into frame. I had Macdonald check the front multiple times. No other vehicles arrived, and we never saw anyone walking. The pair had to have been picked up off the dock via boat.

"Okay. Let's go back to eleven fourteen and try to pause it right when they enter the frame."

"You got it," Macdonald said.

He did as I asked and paused the footage with both men centered on screen. While we couldn't get a clear view of their faces to say with certainty it was Nance and Frost, we had a good view of the guys. Both wore suits. The man leading was taller and slim. We could clearly see that he had longer than shoulder-length hair. The man following was shorter and overweight. He looked bald. The two descriptions fit Frost and Nance enough that I doubted it could be anyone else. We'd seen the footage of Frost and Nance's bodies dropped on the dock in the early hours of Wednesday morning. From the video footage that we were now looking at, we had their whereabouts on Monday night. There was still more than twenty-four hours that we didn't know where they were. We didn't have a printer to get a copy of the still, so I snapped a photo of it with my phone. I brought the photo up to have a look, and it was significantly worse than what the television displayed.

"Let's try to see when the gate was pushed in," I said.

Macdonald switched camera views to the main gate and began to run the footage backward. He used the mouse to click by hour intervals on the recording bar at the bottom of the screen. Hour after hour clicked by. We were in the early Sunday morning hours when the gate went from open to closed between three and four in the morning.

"Play that hour," I said.

Colt and I stood and watched as Macdonald ran the footage. At a quarter to four in the morning, we saw a flash of light from headlights and then a van pushing through the gate.

Macdonald rewound the footage and let it play in real time. The headlights from a van lit the gate. It inched forward until it contacted the bars then pushed through. A single person stepped from the passenger side of the van and pushed the gate all the way open. All we could tell from the video was that the person was tall and big. The description, again, matched everyone that we had involved, and it also matched what we had on Paul Lattore. The man was gloved, his face was covered with something, and the top of his head was obscured by a hat. We weren't getting any identification on the person. After pushing the gate completely open, he hopped into the passenger side and the van backed out. It had never pulled far enough into the driveway for the gate camera to catch the rear of it and get a plate.

"Try to pause it with the van in frame and the guy out of it."

"Sure," Macdonald said, and did.

"What does that look like to you?" I asked. "The van?"

"Minivan. Could be a Honda or Toyota. Kind of hard to tell from the camera's angle," Colt said.

"Yeah, I'm not really up on my minivans," I said. "It doesn't look very old, though." My eyes went to the driver's window of the van. The windows appeared to be tinted. I couldn't even see a shadow of a driver.

"Is there a way that our tech guys can access this?" I asked. "I'd like to try to get some stills from it."

"Sure," Macdonald said. "All they would need is the log-in information, which I can give them."

"Okay." I looked at Colt. "Let me call Wade."

Colt turned his attention to Macdonald. "Can I watch everything once more? I missed some of the beginning."

"No problem," Macdonald said.

I dialed Wade, who picked up after a couple of rings.

"Harrington, what's up?" he answered.

"I've got some more video for you to have a look at."

"Okay. Do you need me to come out to get it from somewhere?" he asked.

"It's cloud-based," I said. "I have someone here who can give you the web address to go to and the log-in to get access."

"Perfect."

"One second." I told Macdonald I had my tech department on the line and passed the phone to him. After he gave Wade all the details, Macdonald handed my phone back.

"Got everything?" I asked.

"Should be all I need," Wade said. "I'll get going on it in just a second. Hey, while I have you on the line, I've got something else here."

"Shoot," I said.

"Well, I got the dimensions from the tower in the boat, and after getting Lattore's height, I got some height and weight estimates on the other two that should be fairly accurate."

"All right."

"Keep in mind, there is some room for error due to a number of things. Obviously one of those being that we can't say with a thousand percent certainty that it actually is Lattore on the boat."

"Rough estimates," I said. "I got it."

"Well, the one guy is actually bigger than Lattore."

"Bigger than Lattore?" I asked.

"Yeah, the guy piloting the boat is no featherweight either. We're looking at around six eight or nine and three hundred-plus on the one guy, and the boat pilot is around six two or three and about two thirty."

"So, including Lattore, we need to find two giants and another big guy?"

"Pretty much," Wade said. "All right. Let me get going on this video."

"Okay, give me an update when you have one," I said.

"Will do."

I ended the call. Movement to my right caught my eye. I glanced over to see Tillerson walking into the kitchen.

CHAPTER 16

Manny

Manny made the turn and glanced up into the rearview mirror of Eric's truck. Justin, driving Paul's Lexus, followed. The street the two traveled looked like it had been left unused for a few years—unused apart from the dumping of unwanted furniture, garbage, and mattresses. Behind a vine-engulfed cement wall, apartments lined the street on the left. The entrance to the apartments was a few blocks away. To the right and behind a chain-link fence were metal buildings in various states of abandon. Green mesh fabric lined the fence and blocked most of the view into the parcel of land. A barbed wire top on the fence assured no unwanted access.

Manny drove past a handful of rusted semi trailers that sat just inside the fence and to a padlocked gate at the dead end, where he put the truck in Park and stepped out. He opened the rear driver's-side door of the truck and pulled out a bolt cutter lying on the floor. Manny swung the door closed while Justin pulled the Lexus up to the gate and waited. Manny went to the lock on the fence, quickly cut it off, and swung the fence door open. Justin pulled through. Manny hopped back in the truck, drove in, then got out to close the gate. Back in the driver's seat, Manny drove toward one of the buildings that had the door open, as per his orders. He looked around the rest of the property. There wasn't much to see other than huge metal buildings filled with garage doors and what looked like an overgrown oval track. Everything around him was in a state of ruin. The blacktop that surrounded each building was gray and crumbled. Weeds, knee high, sprouted through the cracked pavement. Anything metal was rusted. Manny figured the place had been vacant for years.

He pulled the truck inside the building, drove to the far end, turned around, then killed the engine and stepped out. Behind him, Justin did the same. The building resembled a huge metal pole barn. Manny shook his head and looked around. The big doorway that they drove through was the only entrance aside from a pair of service doors—one on the side of the building and one right at their backs. Pigeons flapped around the rafters thirty feet overhead. Some skylights let the only light into the building. Aside from the two vehicles, Justin, Manny, three dead bodies, and the pigeons, nothing else was inside.

"I don't like this," Manny said. "What the hell are we doing here?" He unsnapped the thumb break securing his gun in his shoulder holster. Manny headed to the door behind them and checked it, padlocked from the inside and secure. "Check that door over there."

Justin walked across the building to the side door. Manny

saw him try the handle. Justin turned around and went back. "Locked and has a padlock," he said. Justin rejoined Manny, who stood at the front of the pickup truck.

"Why the hell aren't we just taking care of this?" Manny asked. "Now we need someone else to do it?" Manny furrowed his brow. "We could have Roger bring us a boat and take these three out on the water and send them down."

Justin didn't respond. He kept eyes on the open doorway—the only way in or out unless someone dropped down through a skylight.

"We could have just parked the truck and car in one of the garages at the house. No rush," Manny said. "We could have stripped the cars, sawed them up. Or dumped them down in Liberty City or something. We could have torched them. Since when the hell do we need someone else to dispose of stuff for us?"

"There has to be a reason he wanted it done this way," Justin said.

Manny held up his palms. "I mean we don't even know who the hell we're waiting on," he said.

Again, Justin shrugged. "I stopped asking questions a long time ago. I just do what's asked of me."

"I'm supposed to have the answers to these questions, though. It's kind of my job to know what the hell is going on at all times."

"Why don't you bring it up with Matt?" Justin asked.

Justin didn't get it. And while he and Manny were friends, Justin was nothing more than Matt's glorified servant. He was there with Manny simply because of the sudden opening of positions left by the deaths of Paul and Eric. Justin wasn't in the ranks beneath Manny—his day-to-day normally consisted of sitting by the pool and making drinks, not putting on a gun and doing what needed to be done.

Manny shook his head. He thought about the guy at the warehouse that Matt had met without Manny's knowledge. He thought about the phone call regarding friends down south that Manny had never met or heard of before. He thought about leaving the bodies and how the cops got Paul's name somehow. Something was off. "You haven't seen or heard anything around the house, have you?" Manny asked. "Matt on the phone, people you don't know stopping by? Maybe he and Frank talking about things?"

"Nope," Justin said. "Nothing. Though if the conversation doesn't sound like something I need to hear, or Matt would want me to hear, I usually tune it out or go elsewhere."

Manny questioned whether Justin would have told him even if he had heard something.

They continued to wait. Minutes passed. Matt had told Manny that the contact would be meeting them at eleven sharp. It was ten after. Frank was supposed to show around eleven fifteen to pick up Manny and Justin—Matt had sent him on an errand to one of the carpet-cleaning businesses earlier that morning.

"What are we supposed to do if these guys don't show?" Justin asked.

Manny said nothing. He was still trying to figure out just what the hell was going on—what the angle could be.

"Maybe you should call Matt and see what's up," Justin said. "Let him know whoever we were supposed to be meeting isn't here."

"Yeah," Manny said. He pulled his phone from his pocket and dialed Matt, who picked up in a single ring.

"What's up?" Matt answered.

"Hey, we're sitting here. No one has shown to meet us," Manny said.

"Yeah, he called and said he was running late. He should be there in a couple minutes. Just hang tight."

"Who are we meeting here?" Manny asked.

"The guy's name is David," Matt said.

It wasn't a name that Manny was familiar with.

"Is he coming alone?"

"Yeah," Matt said.

Manny heard Justin snap his fingers and point toward the other end of the big metal building. "That's Frank, right?" Justin asked.

A five-year-old gold Toyota Camry had pulled through the open doorway at the other end of the building and drove toward Justin and Manny.

"Yeah," Manny said. He went back to the call with Matt. "Frank is here."

"Okay. Hey, I have another call coming in. Give me a call on your drive back."

"All right," Manny said. He ended the call and put his phone away.

The Camry pulled to a stop beside the Lexus that Justin had driven. The door opened, and Frank hopped out. He wore a double gun shoulder holster over a black button-down shirt. His normal board shorts were replaced with black slacks that looked almost tactical. The outfit wasn't Frank's normal attire, even when he was out working for Matt.

"Are you guys ready to go?" Frank asked. He walked around the back of the car and came up behind Justin and Manny, who stood at the nose of Eric's pickup truck.

"Nope," Manny said. "This guy hasn't even shown up yet."

Frank rested his elbow on the truck's hood. "Well, what the hell."

Manny grunted in response. "Have you heard of this David guy that we're supposed to be meeting?" Manny looked at Frank for an answer.

"David? Nah, never heard of him," Frank said.

"And what is this place? Why are we meeting this guy here?" Manny asked. He went back to looking at the open doorway at the far end of the building.

"This is an old horse track practice facility," Frank said. "They closed up over here about seven or eight years ago when they expanded the casino. This was one of the stables, or what's left of one. Used to be filled with stalls back in the day."

"Oh," Manny said. "So why are we meeting this guy here?"

"You're not meeting anyone," Frank said.

Manny heard two clicks.

CHAPTER 17

I'd been back at the station for a solid hour. In the time I'd been back, Wade had made a copy of the footage and printed a few stills that he'd brought up to my office. The photos were of two men we assumed were Frost and Nance, and another few shots were of the minivan. Wade seemed pretty confident that it was a 2005 to 2010 Honda Odyssey in silver pearl metallic. We issued a BOLO for the vehicle and a note to look for possible front-end damage. I didn't have a ton of confidence that we were going to find the one we were looking for, yet I had plenty of confidence that we were going to annoy a lot of soccer moms. I imagined there were hundreds, if not more, of similar vans on the streets in the area.

Colt had gotten the Mercedes and Porsche SUV hauled back to our garages at the station. At the house, Tillerson claimed that the Mercedes and Porsche had come from Vice's pool of vehicles and made some phone calls regarding spare keys. We didn't have any luck there, and the last I'd heard, Colt had some local dealerships cutting new ones. Colt said he'd let me know as soon as he'd gotten into the vehicles and started going over them.

Garcia walked into my office with a brown paper sack and a Styrofoam cup. He passed me the bag and set the drink on my desk. He'd gone to grab lunch from Fat Guys, a new burger place down the street from our office.

"Burger, Cajun fries, sweet tea," he said. "As ordered."

"Appreciate it," I said. I opened the bag and pulled out a big foil-wrapped burger. I'd yet to try the place but had heard good things about it from Steve and some of the guys.

"Did you guys already eat?" I asked.

"I ate there, then ordered everyone else's to bring back," Garcia said. He took a seat across from me at my desk and scratched at his short black hair.

I unwrapped the burger, which included a big chunk of lettuce, two patties, tomatoes, grilled onions, ketchup, mustard, and some cheese and pickles—I assumed that was the works that I'd asked for. As I took a big bite and chewed, I had no complaints. As far as burgers went, it was pretty damned good.

"Where are we with everything?" Garcia asked.

I swallowed, got a sip of my tea, and jerked my chin at my computer monitor. "I'm just fishing right now. Looking for anyone in our system of usual suspects that matches our height and weight descriptions that Wade got us."

"And?" Garcia asked.

"And this route is looking like it's going to be a bust," I said. "Nothing that seems to match the giant guy and probably fifty that could match up with the height and weight of whoever was piloting that boat."

"What's going on with Tillerson?"

I reached into the paper bag and got a handful of fries. "He showed up at the house where we found the vehicles and watched the footage. You guys watched it, right? I told Steve to get with Wade on it."

"As soon as Wade had a copy, he called us downstairs to have a look. I can't say there was a ton to see there, but we watched it."

"Okay, good," I said.

"So Tillerson showed up and then what?" Garcia asked.

"Watched the video and that was about it. He didn't have much for us. Wasn't familiar with the house, didn't know of any meeting going down. He did seem to agree that the men on screen were Frost and Nance, though."

"How does he not know every move his undercover guys are making?" Garcia asked.

"Seems it was more of a check-in-weekly kind of thing. I don't know. I imagine that every check-in comes with some risk of keeping a cover. Don't report unless you have something important. They kind of operate on a different system over there."

"Apparently," Garcia said.

"Tillerson said that he was going to meet with Frost's wife sometime today and see if she had anything for us. He was going to let me know."

"You'd have to think that she would know something," Garcia said.

"Maybe not. As far as I know, the undercover guys basically have two separate lives. Nothing intermingles.

Anything that can connect the two lives is a risk of cover."

"I guess that makes sense," Garcia said. "What was going on with the cars themselves?"

"Colt is going to give me a ring as soon as he gets inside them and gets them processed."

My desk phone rang. I took another quick drink of my tea, reached out, and scooped it up. "Harrington."

"It's Halloway. Sounds like we got a pair over in Miami Gardens. We also have Paul Lattore's vehicle on scene, the Lexus that we had a BOLO out for. It's connected."

"What else do we know?" I asked. "Is one of the bodies Lattore?"

"I don't know. This just came through. All I got was that someone called in some suspicious activity and gunshots. Local PD responded and found what they found. It's by the casino and horse tracks."

"All right," I said. "Give me the address, and we'll get over there."

Halloway did, and I wrote it down in my notepad.

I hung the phone back on its base, jammed a quick handful of fries in my mouth, and stood.

"What did we get?" Garcia asked. He rose from the chair and slid it back toward my desk.

"Looks like another two to add to this were just found in Miami Gardens," I said. "A pair of bodies and Paul Lattore's vehicle is on scene. What do you have going on right now?"

"Same as the rest of the guys, waiting around to see if Tech or Forensics comes up with anything. Figured I'd head downstairs to look over Colt's shoulder while he worked."

"You're with me. Let's go."

He gave me a nod and walked from my office. I grabbed Steve and Ryan from the bull pen, and we all headed out—if Colt or Wade got anything to move on, they'd call me. Garcia rode with me. The usual thirty-minute drive took a little longer with midday traffic. I'd sent off a message to Tillerson on the way—I didn't get a response.

We neared the scene a few minutes before one o'clock. My navigation had told me that we'd arrived, yet all I saw was a chain-link fence with some green mesh on our right-hand side. Behind the fence were the tops of some metal buildings. To our left appeared to be some condos or apartments behind a vine-covered wall. I continued down the littered and overgrown road. Around a small bend, I saw a break in the fence just before the dead end. The break was a gate, with a patrol car blocking it. A lone officer stood outside of her car.

I pulled our cruiser up to the patrol car and dropped the window. As the uniformed officer approached, I glanced up into my rearview mirror to see the nose of Steve's cruiser waiting behind us.

"Gentlemen," the officer said.

I looked up, and her name badge read Boddington.

"Lieutenant Harrington, Homicide," I said. "The word is that you guys have something for us."

"Unfortunately," she said. "Two vehicles and two bodies inside one of the metal buildings. My sergeant and a pair of our detectives are in there now with a handful of other officers. You'll see everyone as soon as you're inside. Let me move my car and let you through."

"Thanks," I said.

She moved her vehicle, and we passed through the gate. Large metal pole sheds and buildings littered the immediate landscape. Everything that was made of metal was rusting. Anything painted was fading. Off in the distance, beyond the metal buildings, was what looked like an overgrown racetrack. Some crumbling stands stood off to the side. I figured it had something to do with the horse track at the casino next door—maybe a practice complex that they no longer operated.

"You'd think they'd sell or develop all of this," Garcia said. "This is a big chunk of land to just let sit here."

"Maybe the casino is hanging on to it for expansion or something," I said.

Garcia rocked his head back and forth. "Could be, yeah."

I pulled up and parked next to two patrol cars, an unmarked SUV that had all the signs that it was law enforcement, and three unmarked cruisers in front of a big, faded and rusted tan metal building. Garcia and I left the car, waited for Steve and Ryan, then headed inside through the large open void in the end of the building. On the far end, roughly two hundred feet away, were the vehicles, the officers, and two bodies on the ground.

CHAPTER 18

We handled our introductions with the officers who were on scene. Then we had our initial look around, and I handed out some orders. Steve and Ryan went to talk to the woman who had called in the gunshots and suspicious activity. The word was that she lived on the second floor of one of the condos that we passed coming in. She'd been out on her patio, talking on the phone, when she saw numerous cars heading toward the dead end of the street. A minute or two after they'd passed, she saw the same vehicles driving behind the green fence toward one of the metal buildings. She reported hearing what sounded like gunshots minutes later and then saw a vehicle fleeing the scene.

I stood a few feet from the front of the Lexus sedan that belonged to Lattore. Five feet away, two bodies lay facedown in front of a pickup truck. Each man had taken a single shot to the back of the head from close range. The men also took another pair of shots center mass in the back. The shell casings were left on the scene. Neither man on the ground fit the description for Lattore. One of the guys was slim, his hands and neck covered in tattoos. He had blond hair and couldn't have been much out of his twenties. The other man, Hispanic and in his late thirties or early forties, fit almost exactly the description that we had for the pilot of the boat that left the bodies on the dock—right down to the dreadlocks that were pulled into a ponytail.

"Anything standing out to you?" I asked. The scene and the body positioning didn't make a lot of sense to me. I wanted to know if I was the only one who felt that way or if my observation was shared.

Cliff Downey, the Miami Gardens sergeant who had been leading the scene until we arrived, piped up. "Just the way these two are positioned. They were both facing the doorway." He held his hand out in that direction. "And they both get popped in the back of the head while they were vertical. Took the shots in the back while they were on the ground. Double taps. The thing is, how does someone sneak up behind these guys when they have their backs to nothing but a solid metal corner of a building?"

"This wasn't some kind of kneeling-down execution either," Garcia said. "Bodies would be in a different position if they were kneeling. These guys were standing, but even then, there's still something not quite right. How do two guys get simultaneously shot in the back of the head?"

"Agreed," I said. "If we had one person as a shooter, and these two were standing, you'd think the second guy would have run the moment he heard the first shot. Or hell, at least turned his head and got shot in the face."

I got a nod from one of the Miami Gardens detectives named Ganderton. "Two guys firing at the same time. That or one guy, two guns, same time. The guys weren't expecting it," he said. "But that doesn't mean they were snuck up on."

"Someone, or ones, that they were with," Garcia said.

"Makes sense," Ganderton said. "People standing behind you isn't a big deal if you trust them. They were parked facing the door, as if they were waiting on someone to come in."

"Eyes on the door can't see someone with a gun behind you," said Potts, the other detective, a late forties guy with a gray-and-black mustache.

"Well, Forensics should be able to solve the one- or two-shooter theory," I said. "Let me check on their status." I pulled my phone and dialed Colt. He answered in a few rings and told me that he'd left for our scene twenty minutes prior. As soon as the keys were delivered, Gomez would process the cars belonging to Nance and Frost that were at our garages.

"Forensics should be here in about fifteen minutes," I said while dropping my phone into my pocket. I walked around and got low at each shell casing for a better look—they were all .45 caliber. It could have been from a single gun or a pair of the same caliber. Two different calibers could have told us something. The fact that they were the same didn't tell us much.

I stood and looked over at the Lexus. Something about the way the car sat struck me as odd. I'd noticed the odd stance of the vehicle earlier, but from where I stood at that moment, the sagging rear end of the couple-year-old car was overly pronounced. The car was too new to have failing suspension. Something was in the car's trunk, something heavy. "Did we look through these vehicles at all?"

"We didn't want to touch them," Sergeant Downey said. "You know how the forensics guys are. You touch anything and they ask you why you contaminated their scene."

I nodded. While his statement was true, over the years I'd learned what could and couldn't be touched in the hopes of preserving evidence. Combined with a little common sense, I imagined that I could get a look inside the trunk of the car without disturbing any evidence.

"This thing is, what, a couple years old?" I asked.

"Looks pretty new," Garcia said.

I went to the driver's door of the car and noticed the little black button on the door handle. The car had a smart key feature, so a driver just needed to have the key within a certain proximity to enter and start the car. They also needed to have the key in a certain proximity to the vehicle to pop the trunk, usually by a soft-touch release under the lid. Knowing that, I imagined the interior trunk-release button on the lower part of the driver's-side dash was probably rarely, if ever, used.

"I'm going to grab some gloves from the car," I said. "Be right back."

I walked through the big metal building and to the cruiser we came in. After grabbing a few sets of gloves from the kit in the back, I returned to Garcia at the car and tossed him a pair. I pulled the gloves over my hands and used a single finger to pull the driver's door handle. With my index finger knuckle, I hit the dash button to pop the trunk. When it popped, I stepped to the rear of the car while Garcia was lifting the lid.

"Looks like we just doubled our bodies," Garcia said.

I got a look into the trunk of the car as the other detectives and Sergeant Downey were walking over. Two bodies were stuffed inside. One man large, the other small. While I didn't have a clue who the smaller one was, I was betting the man who looked about three hundred pounds and well over six foot to be Paul Lattore. Both men had been shot in the head. The larger man also looked like he took a couple to the chest. The smaller of the two men, who was covered in dirt and what looked like blood spatter, had no shoes. One of his feet was red with blood and appeared to have had a digit removed.

"What the hell is this?" I asked. I pulled up Lattore's sheet on my phone. The photo we had for him resembled the dead guy in the trunk—minus the bullet hole above his left eye. Hole aside, I was certain it was him. The trunk carpet visible beneath the men looked saturated with blood, and the odor of decomp wasn't yet present—the pair hadn't been dead long.

"I hate to bring it up, but we've got some blood on the rear bumper area of this truck," Detective Potts said.

I took my eyes from the two bodies in the trunk and glanced over at the detective.

Potts stood two feet from the back of the pickup truck and held a flashlight's beam on the tailgate. "It looks like it's leaking from something in the bed," he said.

I walked over, and Garcia followed. The sergeant and Detective Ganderton had already taken up positions at Potts's shoulders.

"Did you want to try getting in here?" Sergeant Downey asked.

I used a finger to pull the handle for the gate and guided it down as I stared at the soles of a pair of dress shoes. They were huge, as was the man that they belonged to. I tried the handle at the top of the hard tonneau cover and let the hydraulic shocks raise it. We got ourselves a good look at the man. While I didn't recognize him, he fit the description of someone who was larger than Lattore. The guy was bald with a big beard. He'd been shot in the head like the other two men lying at the front of the truck.

I glanced over at the open trunk of the Lexus and then between the two cars at the two men lying dead in front of them. I didn't have any answers. The only leads we had up to that point centered around a group of people who were all dead around me in the building where I stood. Who the hell killed them, and why, I didn't know. Who the other two deceased were, I didn't know either.

CHAPTER 19

Frank

Frank pulled the Camry into the parking lot of the business off Northwest 104th Street—the production center or Hialeah Gardens location. Of the four carpet-cleaning businesses, three were distribution centers and only one was where the product was made.

Frank found a parking spot in the empty lot and dialed John, who Matt had recently appointed to oversee production and distribution. Three rings later, John answered.

"Hello," John said.

"It's Frank."

"Frank. How are you doing?"

"Good, good. How are we looking on collection?"

"Everything should be here within the hour, I'd think. All the money from Miami Gardens and Carol City. I'll get it all loaded up in a van and ready to go as soon as it arrives."

"Perfect," Frank said. He reached over into the Camry's glove compartment, opened it, and pulled out a pair of suppressors. Frank pinned the phone to his ear with his shoulder and removed one of his pistols from his holster. He screwed on the suppressor then repeated the process with his other weapon. "I'll be there in around an hour. If something changes, call me."

"Will do. And remember my two hundred bucks," John said with a laugh.

"Two hundred bucks?"

"From cards last week," John said. "You know, when you went all in with a four-nine offsuit."

"I would have looked like a million bucks stealing that pot." Frank chuckled. "Yeah, I got your money. Don't worry about it."

"I wasn't. Just giving you shit. See you in an hour."

"Sounds good," Frank said. He ended the call and replaced each gun into its holster. He grabbed his suit jacket from the passenger seat and stepped from the car. Frank pulled the jacket on while he looked around. No one was in sight. He remembered when he'd selected the location and how perfect he thought it was. The carpet-cleaning building was stand-alone, roughly six thousand square feet, and located on a dead-end street in a giant industrial area. Directly south, across the street, was the rear of a printing factory that took up the entire block. Aside from a small covered area where employees gathered to smoke near the railroad tracks a few hundred feet east, there was never a soul out back of the place. On the building's side of the road, to the north and east, were two industrial scrap yards. To the west was an industrial crane business that had a fenced-in lot. Foot traffic coming into the store wasn't an issue. Most days, the Open sign was never turned around.

Frank headed to the front door. Four cars were parked near the back of the lot—one of them he recognized as belonging to Keith, the lead cook.

A plastic Closed sign hung on the glass door. Frank hit the bell and waited. He looked up at the camera pointed at him. A minute or two passed with no one answering. Frank hit the bell again then banged on the door with the butt of his fist. He had keys for the place back in the car. Frank turned to get them. Ten feet from the front door, he heard it open behind him. He turned around to see Keith, dressed in a white coat and with a respirator draped from his neck, hanging out the door.

"What's up?" Keith asked.

Frank turned around and went toward the entrance. "Get your ass inside," Frank said. "Standing out here like an idiot."

Keith retreated into the building, and Frank followed.

"Lock the door," Frank said.

Keith did and then walked to the store's front counter.

"What the hell is wrong with you?" Frank asked. "Answering the door in lab gear. What are you, stupid?"

"Sorry, man. I was cleaning up the lab. We just finished a cook that Matt ordered a couple hours ago. The bell about scared the shit out of me. I went to the cameras and saw that it was you out here, so I came to get the door."

"Use your head. What if someone drove by and you're standing out front like that?"

Keith pulled the respirator from around his neck and tossed it on the front counter.

"It won't happen again," Keith said. "I wasn't thinking."

"Yeah, I know," Frank said.

"So, uh, what's up?" Keith asked. He was late twenties, thin, and wore his hair half covering his face, which required a flick of his head every few seconds for him to see. Keith was a freelance meth-cooking whiz, and Matt hired him to try his hand at cooking Krokodil. Matt gave him a truckload of cash to get a lab up and running in the carpet-cleaning store. Not a user, Keith had been a damn reliable employee.

"I'm just checking in," Frank said. "Matt has me popping into all the stores today."

"You can let him know that we should be able to push out about three fifty this week and move up from there. Four shouldn't be a problem next week," Keith said. "And if you could, tell him that the slowing-of-production thing was never because of me or what we could put out. I got the order from Jaime that we needed to dial back a bit. Getting the codeine is really the only thing that's keeping us from getting close to that five hundred number. We should be able to do four plus without a problem. And it sounds like John is able to move more than Jaime had been."

"That's all fine. I'll let him know," Frank said. "Who all is here?"

"Me and a couple of workers," Keith said.

"Specifically," Frank said.

"A guy named Nick, another named Toby, another that goes by Haavi. Three workers and myself."

"Okay. You said you just finished the cook?"

"A few hours ago, yeah. We're still packaging."

"Show me," Frank said.

Keith waved Frank to follow and stepped past the front desk, a supply closet, and a restroom, and then into the warehouse. The floor space for the trucks was a quarter of the size of any of the other stores. Two vans were parked inside the building—all that would fit. Commercial shelving units, twenty feet high, rose to the exposed rafters on each side of the vans. Jugs of chemicals for the carpet-cleaning trade, and boxes containing more of the same, filled the shelves. To the left, opposite the vans and garage doors, were three offices. The offices were similar—a desk with papers scattered across it, no phones or computers, random photos and certifications filling the big built-in bookshelves. Each office had white walls with miscellaneous business-related posters affixed to them. Keith walked to the last office in the line.

Frank had yet to see any of the workers that Keith had said were present. "Is everyone in the lab?"

"Yeah. They're getting the product packaged," Keith said. He entered the office and went to the built-in bookshelf farthest right. Keith pushed on the shelf—filled with photos, books, and paperweights—and the entire thing swung inward. Frank followed him through the doorway created by the bookshelf and into the lab. The bookshelf door was a readily available unit, yet with the rest of the offices built to have similar looking bookshelves, no one would ever guess that it was a door. The pass-through was the only entrance into the hidden twenty-by-thirty-foot room. When Frank and Matt built the room, Frank thought for certain that from inside, someone would be able to tell that its footprint didn't match the size and shape of the building from the outside. Yet without windows in the warehouse to begin with, it was all but impossible.

Keith closed the bookshelf doorway.

Frank looked to his left at all the stainless steel vats, equipment, and shelving filled with supplies to create the product. A six-foot-tall spray dryer stood alone in the corner. He'd never once watched a cook. The truth was, he didn't care how the stuff was made, but he knew the general idea of the process going on in the lab. Codeine was mixed with a bunch of other garbage and chemicals—mainly paint thinner, gas, acid, iodine, and red phosphorous. The final milky yellow liquid was dried then packaged for transport. After transport, it turned into the final product, the only thing Frank and Matt cared about—money. The drugs were simply a means to that end. Frank turned his head to the right to see two men wearing lab coats and masks who were packaging a dingy tan, almost brown powder at a table at the back of the room. Next to it, another man in similar attire weighed the product on a big scale that hung from the ceiling. From the small bit of remaining powder and stack of packaged drugs, Frank imagined them to be almost done.

Keith started walking to the men at the packaging table.

Frank didn't move from the room's only exit. He reached into his jacket and removed the pistol under his left arm.

"Hey, what the hell," one of the men said. He'd seen Frank draw his weapon.

The guy grabbed the man beside him, who was also

packing the product, by the shoulder.

Keith turned to see what was happening behind him. Frank took aim on Keith and squeezed a pair of rounds into Keith's chest. In the enclosed cinder block room, even with the suppressor, the rounds from the gun made an earsplitting crack. As Keith's body dropped, Frank moved the barrel of his pistol a few inches to the right, got aim on the man who first noticed the gun, and fired another two shots. He watched the man drop as he drew aim on the man at the scale.

The guy at the scale immediately flipped the table next to him, sending a cloud of powder into the air, and took cover behind it. Frank saw the other man who'd been packaging the product scrambling to get behind the stainless steel table as well.

Frank smirked at their pathetic attempt at prolonging their lives a few more seconds. He reached his left hand into his jacket and removed his other pistol. Frank took aim on the three-by-five-foot table and put a single shot through it. A split second later, a man leapt from the cover of the table and scrambled to get behind a drum of gasoline ten feet away. Frank swung his gun toward the man but didn't shoot. He trained the weapon back on the table and put another round into it. The man behind it sprang up and put his hands into the air. Frank put a pair in the guy's wide-open chest.

He swung his weapon toward the drum of gasoline. "Come out, shithead," Frank said.

"I didn't do anything," the guy said.

Frank took another step into the room and tried to crane his neck for a look at the guy hiding behind the drum. While Frank wasn't certain the men weren't armed, he imagined that he would have received return fire if they were.

"I'm going to spill this barrel," the guy said. "Light it up. With all the shit in here, you won't be able to get out before everything bl—"

Frank fired a single round through the upper center section of the barrel before the guy could finish his threat. The man flopped out face-first on the cement. Frank took aim on the guy's head and squeezed off another round. Gasoline spilled from the hole and splashed the floor of the lab. The fuel mixed with the blood pooling beneath the guy.

Frank walked man-to-man and double tapped each before heading over to the packaged drugs. He took a pair of gloves from a nearby box and slipped them on. He wasn't much concerned with the spilling fuel. Frank started gathering the drugs that Matt had ordered—the Krokodil would be leaving with him.

CHAPTER 20

I held my cell phone to my ear.

"Hey, I got your text. What do you have?" Tillerson asked.

I looked at the bodies that Colt and Skip had laid in a line. "Every lead or person of interest that we knew about dead and laid out in front of me. One of them looks like Lattore. One we're thinking is an Eric Rossi, judging by the size of the guy. Well, that and the plates of a truck sitting here come back to him. One looks to be the guy who was piloting the boat that dropped the bodies on the dock. We're going to have to dig into these guys and try to find out something."

"What's the scene look like?" Tillerson asked.

"Two dead, at the front of a vehicle. GSWs. Head shots and what look like double taps after they were down. In the building that they're in, it would appear as if they were waiting for someone. Backs to the wall and facing the only entrance. We had those two dead there, Lattore and another guy were stuffed into the trunk of Lattore's Lexus, and the one we figure to be Eric Rossi was found in the bed of his truck."

"Somehow I'm not understanding that picture when I try

to visualize it. Were these guys put in the trunk on scene?"

"It doesn't appear that three of the five were killed here, no."

"But we think that three of these guys were together for the body drop of Frost and Nance?"

"Three of the five, yeah," I said.

"Yet Lattore and the other big guy, who we had on that boat dumping Nance and Frost, are dead in the backs of vehicles, but the guy we figured was piloting the boat is dead outside of the vehicles?" Tillerson asked.

"Correct," I said.

Silence came from his end of the phone.

"Here's my thinking. The two big guys, Lattore and Rossi, along with the other mystery guy, with missing digits, were killed somewhere else and brought here by these other two. Who killed those guys, we don't know."

"Okay. I think I understand. What about IDs on the three we don't know?" Tillerson asked.

"We're going to get into the pockets of the other guys here in a second. Forensics just got their pictures and saw them as found, and now we're going to see if they have any ID on them. Worst case, we can print them on scene before they're taken to the ME's office."

"Think someone knew we were after these guys, and put them away?" Tillerson asked.

It was logical, and at that point, I hadn't put any thought into the motive for these guys meeting their ends. Yet the only way that someone could have known we were looking into the men was if they were getting inside information on the investigation. And that wasn't something that I wanted to think about at the moment. "Could be," I said. "We'll have to see what shakes out."

"Okay. Well, I may have something here. I found a file Frost put together on this investigation he and Nance were on."

"Where did you find a file?"

"His wife found it at their house. She claimed that Frost disappeared into the garage for a while every time he came home. It was a thing. She was supposed to just give him his time in there. She remembered hearing the ladder a couple times. This morning, she started looking for whatever was in there. She found a locked trunk in the attic and took a hammer to it. Inside was his wedding ring, his wallet with his true ID, and his credit cards. That and a file. The last entry is five days old. It was from the last time he'd come home. It mentions a guy named Tavaras. Seems he was trying to put together a meeting between Frost and whoever was manufacturing the Krokodil."

"Tavaras?" I asked. "Is that a first or last name?"

"Last. Carlos Tavaras. He goes by Big T on the streets. The guy is a known upper-level pusher. And the name is a misnomer. He's like five foot one and not much more than a hundred pounds soaking wet. I have people out looking for him as we speak."

I put eyes on the man missing a finger and toe beside Lattore's giant body.

"I think I may know where he is. And I have a feeling that we're not going to have much luck questioning him," I said. I took the mouthpiece of the phone from my face. "Someone pull a sheet on a guy named Carlos Tavaras," I said. "And if we can start checking for IDs on these guys, let's do it."

Detective Potts said he would run the name. Garcia went to Colt, who said he'd start digging through pockets. I went back to the call.

"You think he's one of your DBs there?" Tillerson asked.

"Fits the height and weight description of the guy missing digits. I have one of the local detectives pulling the guy's sheet now. What else does it say about him?"

"Not much. Just that he mentioned something about the Krokodil being distributed through a carpet-cleaning business."

"Carpet-cleaning business?" I asked. "Something local?"

"Don't know. That's it. Frost's notes say that he was looking into a couple businesses but hadn't made any headway, and nothing is listed by name in the file. He wrote that he didn't want to press Tavaras for more, figuring it could jeopardize the possible meeting with whoever was behind the curtain."

"Maybe it would have been better if it had," I said. I caught Steve and Ryan walking toward the building. They stopped just before entering, and Steve was pointing at something off in the distance. "I'm going to get back into this, Tillerson. Are you coming out here?"

"No. I'm driving now. On my way to meet Nance's brother. It doesn't sound like he has anything for us, but I'm going to have a talk with him either way. Seems they both visited their mother together last week. You never know,

Nance could have said something to him in passing that slipped his mind."

"All right. I'll send you a message when we get positive IDs on these guys."

"Sure," he said. "I'll get a copy of this file made for you and put it on your desk as soon as I get back."

"Appreciate it," I said.

"I'll be in touch."

I ended the call and gave my attention to Steve and Ryan. "What's the story from our witness?"

"Says she was on her patio when two vehicles, a truck and a car, entered this property and pulled into this building."

"She had a clear view?" I asked.

"Perfect," Ryan said. "She showed us the view from her balcony. You can see the street and then, over the fence, pretty much everything back here. Can't really say that a bunch of rusty buildings make for an appealing view, but in this instance, it couldn't have been any better."

"So, the truck and car come in, and then what?"

"A gold sedan, Camry, she says, drives down the road and enters the property here," Steve said. "Pulls into this building with the other vehicles. She says a minute or so later, she hears what sounds like a couple gunshots and then sees the car drive out. She said it looked like it was driving fast."

"Do we have anything better than gold Camry?" I asked. "Approximate year?"

"I showed her a couple body styles on my phone, but she couldn't be a hundred percent. Anything from a 2002 to 2016. The Camry matches up with what Frost's neighbor had mentioned he saw the guys posing as cops driving."

"Yeah, it does. Except we think those guys are here, dead. Did he give a year?"

"I think he just said, like, five years old," Steve said.

"All right. What about people inside? Did she see how many?"

Steve shook his head.

"Okay. So gold Camry. Maybe five years old, that is, if it's the same vehicle. Gotta be a few hundred or more on the streets in the area. I don't think that's going to break this case. She didn't have anything else other than what you just said?" I asked.

"That was the extent of it," Steve said.

"That's him. Carlos Tavaras," Detective Potts called out.

I looked past Steve at Potts, still fifty feet away and walking toward us. "I have his photo here," Potts said.

The detective walked to our group and showed me his phone, which had an image of Carlos Tavaras's DL. Our DB bore enough of a resemblance to make it all but a certainty that it was him that came from the trunk. "Thanks, Potts," I said.

"How did we get a name to look up?" Steve asked.

"Tillerson on the phone," I said. "He found a file that Frost put together on the investigation he and Nance were working. Carlos Tavaras, that little guy there, was mentioned in it. He was trying to arrange a meeting between Frost and whoever was behind the drugs."

"Anything else in the file?" Ryan asked.

"A carpet-cleaning business is mentioned as the company

the drugs were possibly being distributed through. No names. No locations. Doesn't say if this is a local thing or not."

CHAPTER 21

Garcia had been digging through pockets and wallets with Colt. He walked to Garcia, Steve, and me, who were checking out the pickup truck left on scene.

"What did we get?" I asked.

Garcia looked down at a notepad he held. "All of them had wallets and IDs. Carlos Tavaras was the little one missing a finger and toe. Sounds like we got that already. Then we have an Eric Rossi, the owner of this truck, and Paul Lattore, the owner of the Lexus. I think we were pretty certain on all those guys. Our two mystery men. The blond guy with the tattoos there is Justin Staley. Age thirty-one, hair blond, eyes blue, five foot ten and one sixty-one. Address in West Miami."

"And him?" I asked and pointed my chin at the thick-framed Hispanic guy with the dreads in a ponytail.

"Manuel Jimenez. Two twenty-eight and six foot one. Age forty. North Miami Beach address. The other detective, Ganderton, is running all the names for priors."

"I'm betting it's probably safe to say these guys are going to have laundry lists of offenses. We're going to have to dig

143

into each of these guys and see just what if anything we can find out. Maybe we can tie one of the guys back to a carpet-cleaning business somehow."

"Carpet cleaning?" Garcia asked.

"Yeah. There was a mention of it in Frost's file," I said.

"That Manuel Jimenez has a receipt for a carpet-cleaning store in his wallet. I literally just looked at it," Garcia said. "It's for, like, a dollar and some change."

"That doesn't strike me as coincidental," Steve said.

"Show me," I said.

Garcia turned toward Colt, who was at the bodies, and began walking to him. "Hey, Colt. What did we do with the wallet from this one?" Garcia pointed toward Manuel Jimenez's body.

"Bagged in my tote," Colt said. "Do we need it?"

"Yeah," I said. "I need to see where the receipt for the carpet-cleaning place came from."

"One second." Colt stood from his kneeling position at Justin Staley's body, where he'd been snapping photographs of the man's tattoos. Colt let the camera hang from his neck and walked to the big gray tote with the open top. He reached in and removed a sealed, clear plastic evidence bag. Colt ripped the top of the bag open and removed the wallet. He fished the receipt from between some bills and held it up. He turned it so I could get a look.

I took a step forward and focused on the receipt's writing. It had come from a place called The Carpet Cleaners. The business name left something to be desired in the originality department. "Someone pull the name of this place up," I said. "Let's see where the hell it is."

"Hold on," Steve said.

I watched him punch the name of the business into his phone. A search result listed the company's website at the top of the results, followed by a map of all the local locations. There appeared to be four inside the greater Miami area.

"All within twenty minutes or so of here," Steve said.

"Colt, what do you have going on out here?" I asked.

"I'd like to finish with my photographs and then move on to the vehicles. Give them a once-over and get some pictures there. I planned to spread out after that. Get some of the building. And then it's prints—"

"Timewise," I said, cutting him off.

"Probably a couple hours, honestly," he said.

"Can you hold down the fort? Maybe call someone from the office out?" I asked.

"Yeah. If you have something to move on, go do it," Colt said. "This ain't my first rodeo. If I find something or need you for anything, I'll call."

"You sure?" I asked.

"Catch ya later," Colt said. He brought his camera up to his eye and snapped another photo of the bodies.

"All right." I had a look at Steve's phone and divided the four locations among us. Garcia and I were going to take the stores in Miramar and Gladeview. Steve and Ryan were taking the stores in Carol City and Hialeah Gardens. We'd meet back at the station after that. We left Colt with the scene right around a quarter to three.

Our first stop was the Miramar location. The drive from Miami Gardens was only four miles but took us almost fifteen minutes with traffic. Down the block, a yellow-and-black sign reading "The Carpet Cleaners" was on a pole by the street. I hung a right and turned in to the business's lot.

"This place looks closed," Garcia said as he scratched at his black goatee.

I pulled into a spot a few feet away from the building's front doors and had a look at the place. A few windows surrounded the front door of a big square tan metal building. The landscaping consisted of cement, and no lights were on inside. I looked around the parking lot, which could have probably held twenty cars. Three cars were parked toward the back corner of the building near the garage doors. One was a ten-year-old sport utility, one was a small pickup truck, and one was a sedan. None were the minivan or Camry that we'd been after.

"Let's give the door a knock and see what we get," I said.

We left the car and walked to the building's entrance. As suspected, a Closed sign hung inside the front glass door. The hours were listed on a separate sign to the right of the door's handle. The business was closed Mondays and Sundays—it was neither.

"Supposed to be open," I said. I cupped my hands around my face and got a look inside. The front of the building had a small show floor. A few carpet displays were on the walls, and what looked like rental machines were lined up against the back wall near some supply shelves. I spotted a front counter and a cash register off to my right. From what I saw of the footprint of the building from the outside, I imagined that beyond the front desk was a warehouse where they kept the vans.

"Maybe they're at lunch," Garcia said.

I tried the door, which was locked, then banged on the glass with my fist. Maybe someone was inside, just not in the showroom. No one came to the door.

"Let's go knock on those garage doors," Garcia said.

I pointed toward the back of the building and followed him.

Garcia gave the door two good raps with his fist, and we waited.

I didn't hear a peep—no voices, no rummaging around, nothing.

"Where's the other store?" I asked.

"About fifteen miles south in Gladeview," Garcia said. "That's got to be a good half hour-plus drive right now." He balled his fist and gave the metal garage door a few more knocks. Again, we waited, and again, no one came.

The sun was bearing down on us and made Garcia swipe the sweat from his forehead into his black hair. "You ready?" he asked.

"Yeah, let's run the tags on these cars and then head over to check that other place out. This place looks pretty quiet."

Garcia agreed, and he pulled his notepad from the inner pocket of his gray suit jacket. He took down the three tag numbers on the cars, and we walked to our unmarked cruiser. I ran the tags while Garcia kept eyes on the building for any movement. Two of the tags came back to the men registered as owners—a Hector Velez and a Howard Portnow. The third vehicle, the sport utility, was registered to a Rosanna Kimmel. We ran the three owners for priors.

One of the men and the woman had previous drug charges—a possession on the man and a possession with intent on the woman. The other man, Velez, came back clean.

I dialed Steve to see what kind of luck he and Ryan were having.

"Any luck?" I asked when Steve answered.

"We just left our first one that we checked out," Steve said. "The place was closed."

"So was ours," I said. "Did you get a look inside?"

"Yeah, nothing looked off. It just looked like they were closed for the day. They were supposed to be open, though, judging by the sign on the door," Steve said.

"Same thing we found," I said. "Business hours say open. Locked door and lights off say closed."

"Well, that all sounds about right," Steve said. "Ryan was going through the reviews from the place that were posted online. Two out of five stars average. Quite a few of the reviews mention the place being closed when customers pull on the door. That and being backlogged for weeks. Yet, thinking about it, how much foot traffic do you think these places actually get? Seems to me like more of a call or book-online kind of thing."

"Could be," I said. "Any cars out at the place you came from?"

"Just a pair. Volvo wagon and a Hyundai sedan. We ran the tags. Ryan has the names of the owners, but we didn't see anything too interesting. A DUI and a drug charge on the one. An old assault charge on the other."

"Our results were similar. Two of our three over here had previous drug charges."

"Hmm. What do you make of that?" Steve asked.

"Not sure yet. We were just about to head south to the other one and see if we have better luck. We may need to dig into these names further when we get back, see what else we can find."

"Okay," Steve said. "We'll check in after our next stop if we don't hear from you first."

"Sounds good," I said.

I ended the call and fired up the cruiser's motor.

"See any movement?" I asked.

"Nothing," Garcia said.

"All right. Let's roll." I put the cruiser in Reverse and backed from the parking spot. "Pull this next place up on a map."

"They didn't get anything over there either?" Garcia asked as he searched the address of the next carpet-cleaning store.

"Seemed to me like they got pretty much the same thing as we got over here. Vehicles in the lot there come back to owners with drug priors, though. I don't imagine it's a coincidence."

"Probably not."

I waited at the parking lot's exit for Garcia's directions. "Right or left?"

"Sorry. Make a right," he said.

I did, and we headed up the street. With a few directions coming from the speaker of his phone, we made our way to the turnpike and headed south.

CHAPTER 22

Frank

Frank gave the front door two taps with his knuckle and waited for John, who was at the front counter, to walk over and unlock the door. Bells sounded when John pulled it open.

"Did you drive one of the vans?" John asked.

"Yeah," Frank said. He didn't elaborate. Prior to leaving the lab, he'd loaded the back of the van with all the drugs that had just been cooked.

"Okay. Well, you've got perfect timing," John said.

Frank followed John inside the building, and John turned the lock on the front door behind him. The sound of music coming from the warehouse filled the room.

"The Carol City guys just left, and we've got everything being loaded up as we speak," John said.

"Good," Frank said. "Who all is here?"

"Me, Eddie, Rey, and Clint."

"So, the money is loaded up?"

"Should be just about ready to go, yeah." John motioned

for Frank to follow him and spoke over his shoulder as he went to the back. The volume of the music grew with each step. "When did you want to play next?" he asked. "I've got a couple of guys that have been begging for a game. Real donkeys. Should make for some easy money."

Frank drew his pistol and lifted it to the bald spot on the back of John's head. He popped off a single round just as John reached for the keypad on the metal door. Blood spattered the wall and door, and John fell face-first to the floor.

From his pocket, Frank pulled a pair of nitrile gloves that he'd taken from the lab and slipped them on. He put two rounds into John's back and, with a gloved fingertip, punched the six-digit code into the access door to the warehouse. He stepped into the room and snapped his head to the right. Eddie and Rey, who obviously hadn't heard the suppressed gunshots over the music, sat on the back bumper of one of the vans, eating their lunch. Frank drew aim on Eddie just as they locked eyes. Eddie dropped his bagged sandwich, and Frank put a pair into his chest. Eddie fell into the van.

Frank panned his aim left for Rey, a short, wide grunt who had been doing manual labor for the crew. Rey sprung up, sending a plastic lunch box flying, as he made a break for cover. Frank squeezed off two rounds, both missing and punching holes through the rear metal wall of the building. Rey wasn't as lucky with the next rounds fired. Frank saw Rey's body contort and drop. Rey skidded a foot or two across the concrete before coming to rest. Frank stepped over to the two guys and put another two rounds into each. Clint was the only one missing. Even with the music playing and the suppressed gun, Frank found it hard to believe Clint wouldn't have heard the gunshots inside the warehouse.

When Frank yanked the plug from the socket on the wall, the radio went silent. His eyes shot around the room. The offices taking up one wall were all dark, yet Frank walked over for a better look. Neither of the offices offered a place to hide—neither had a closet, and Clint couldn't hide under the desks facing the wall either. He hadn't seen Clint in the front showroom, which meant that he was hiding in a storage room, a restroom, or one of the four vans.

Each van had its rear doors open, allowing Frank to see into the cargo area, yet a metal wall prevented him from seeing if anyone was in the passenger compartments. Frank headed to the vans as he dropped the magazine from his gun, replaced it with another from a cargo pocket on his pants, then removed his second pistol. He neared the passenger door of the last van in line and got a look. He saw no one inside, yet he couldn't see if someone was hiding along the floor without either stepping up to look or opening the door—neither of which he'd be doing. Frank placed the barrel of his gun to the truck's passenger door around the level of the footwell and fired a pair of shots. He listened, heard nothing, and moved on to the next van. At each van, he did the same thing. He went back through each to check after he'd made it past the last one—no one had been hiding inside. In between vans, Frank had been dropping to see if anyone was underneath or trying to sneak away. He'd been keeping eyes on the doors for the storage room and restroom. He'd yet to see any motion anywhere.

Frank went to the storage room—basically, a walled-off closet that held some cleaning supplies, a mop bucket, and a utility sink. The walls were studs and drywall, and the door was hollow-core wood. Frank wouldn't have to go inside to check. He brought both pistols up and swept rounds left to right. Eight shots total. He listened but heard nothing. No moans, no groans, no crashing around, and no body dropping.

The only hiding spot left was the restroom. Frank moved the aim of his guns to the bathroom's closed door. The moment he did, it burst open. In a full run, Clint came straight at Frank. Frank fired repeatedly. Clint didn't get five feet outside the door before landing face-first on the cement. He was dead before he hit the floor. Frank holstered his weapons and headed to the next office. Inside, he yanked the hard drive for the cameras as he'd done at the other locations—Frank had installed the security and knew precisely where each recording unit was. He left the office for the vans. Frank was going to try to stuff every bag of money and every bag of drugs into his van outside. It all needed to go back to the house. Business was closed, and he and Matt were relocating.

CHAPTER 23

I stood at the front door of the carpet-cleaning store, looking into the locked showroom. The building, like the others, had a Closed sign on the door when the listed hours indicated they should have been open. There were no lights on inside and no people. We'd run the tags on the four cars in the lot, and just like the others that had been run, the registered owners had questionable pasts.

"Let's go bang on the garage," I said.

As Garcia and I walked to the building's dual garage doors, my cell phone buzzed in my pocket.

I slid it out and answered—Steve was calling.

"What's up," I said.

"I think I'm looking at our Camry. Hell of a coincidence if it's not."

"What? Where? At the carpet-cleaning store?"

I watched as Garcia banged on the garage door with a closed hand.

"Yeah, and this place is in the middle of nothing," Steve said. "Train yards, trucking depots, and factories. Odd location for a carpet-cleaning business when all the other

154

ones are in a retail setting. We're waiting on local backup before we try to see exactly what the hell is going on here."

"All right. Any other cars there?" I asked.

"Looks like four cars here and the Camry. We haven't run any of the plates, though. We drove past, saw the Camry, and drove back the way we came for another look. The color matches, obviously. I think it would be too damn coincidental to not be connected."

"Okay. What's the situation right now?"

"We just pulled to the side of the road over here where we can keep eyes on the place. I dialed you. Ryan called for the local PD. That's where we're at. We've been on scene here for a total of about a minute."

"Okay. Hang tight. We're going to make our way over there in a second. We'll run the plates on the cars here, double-check that no one is inside, and roll. Call me with any news."

"You got it," Steve said.

I ended the call and dumped my phone into my pocket. "They got the Camry at the store in Hialeah Gardens."

"Okay," Garcia said. From his single-word answer, he seemed distracted. He leaned closer to the garage door with his ear next to it. "It sounds like someone is in there," he said. His words were quiet, just above a whisper.

I motioned him away from the door and put my back to the cinder block of the building beside it. I leaned closer, trying to get a listen, but didn't hear anything. "Go try to get a look around the back. Maybe there's a window or something."

Garcia nodded and walked to the back corner of the building.

I banged on the garage door again yet still heard no noise coming from inside. We needed to go, to get over to the other business where Ryan, Steve, and the Camry were.

"Body, body, body," Garcia said, rounding the corner. He had his service weapon in hand.

"There's a guy on the floor inside. The lights are on." Garcia approached me beside the garage door.

As I pulled my weapon from my holster, I heard an engine fire up inside the building. The sound was followed by the immediate squeal of tires. I grabbed Garcia by the front of his suit jacket and yanked him toward me. The nearest garage door, just feet from us, exploded outward over the nose of a van. The van slid sideways in the parking lot and drove over the garage door it threw from its nose. I drew on it and fired, but it kept moving. The van slammed into the front corner of our unmarked cruiser, sending it spinning and slamming into a nearby concrete pylon that held a light pole. The van threw dirt and grass in the air as it made its way across the landscaping and shrubs at the sidewalk in front of the building. The van bounced into the street, sending bits of plastic and debris flying, before righting itself and heading up the block.

I ran for our cruiser with Garcia on my heels, but twenty feet away from our car, I knew our chances at a pursuit were over. The front right tire of our car was blown out from being hit—ripped away from the rim. The front driver's side was embedded around the waist-high concrete pillar. A puddle of coolant rolled from beneath the car. "Son of a bitch!"

I ran out to the street with my gun aimed in the direction the van had fled. I caught a view of it, two blocks down, making a hard right at the next intersection.

"Did you get a look at whoever was in the van?" I asked. I turned toward Garcia.

"Not even a glimpse," he said.

"Keep a gun on that door," I said.

Garcia did, and I yanked my phone from my pocket to call 911.

"911, what's your emergency?" a female voice asked.

I gave the dispatcher my information and location and requested immediate support in locating the van. After giving her the van's last known direction, I told her we'd need the police at our current location. She tried to keep me on the line, but I hung up, stuffed my phone in my pocket, and walked to the building. We needed to get inside and get the place cleared.

Garcia and I entered the garage door void into a warehouse. The wall to our left was shelving units filled with jugs of chemicals. To the right was the back metal wall of the building and more shelving. Three vans, identical to the one that just went crashing out the garage door, sat parked door-to-door in the center of the warehouse. We went from one to the next. Each van appeared to have bullet holes in the front passenger door—why, I hadn't a clue. The backs of each were open, and two of the three were empty. The third van had a deceased male inside. Blood was spattered on the rear interior of the door—more of it was in the empty cargo area. It looked like he might have been in the middle of eating, judging by the spilled cooler and bloody sandwich on the ground within arm's reach.

My eyes went to the body that I figured Garcia had spotted from outside. The man lay facedown fifteen feet from the rear of the vans. His head faced away. A small blood pool came from his midsection. Garcia went to him, checked for a pulse, and shook his head. We continued.

The wall opposite the garage doors held two offices, a closed door, and a restroom. A few feet from the open restroom door was another body. The man, thin with short spiked blond hair, looked like he'd taken a number of bullets. A single shell casing lay beside him, and another was on his back.

Garcia got my attention by snapping his fingers. He pointed at the wall beside the restroom that held the closed door. We walked over. Bullet holes filled the wall. More spent shell casings littered the floor. I pulled the door open, and Garcia cleared the small cleaning closet—nothing but brooms, cleaning supplies, and mop buckets.

We continued to the offices and then toward a metal door that led into the front of the building. More shell casings were on the floor near the door.

I turned the door's handle and stopped the second I pushed it open. The entire wall to my right was covered in blood spatter. At my feet was another body, a man who'd clearly taken a shot to the back of his head at close range. The man lay facedown, and his face was inches from the wall. A good portion of the exit wound took up the better half of the left side of his face. I pushed the door open as far as it would go, and Garcia went through. I followed him, feeling the squish of the blood-saturated carpet. Another pair of offices, another restroom, and the show floor were quickly cleared. No one was breathing in the building aside from Garcia and myself.

I holstered my weapon, as did Garcia.

"What the hell just happened in here?" I asked.

"The guy or guys in the van were probably our shooters," Garcia said.

"Get on the phone with the local PD and see what the hell is going on with getting this van," I said. "If we need to get a bird up, let's get it up."

"Got it," Garcia said.

I dialed Steve.

"Hey," he answered. "We're still waiting. The car hasn't moved. Are you guys on your way?"

"No," I said. "Someone just tried running us down. Came smashing out of the garage of the carpet-cleaning store here in one of the company vans and took out our cruiser. We've got four bodies inside the building."

"What the hell," Steve said. "Who was in the van?"

"We don't know," I said. "Took out our car and fled. We don't even know how many people were in it. I made the call to the locals right away. Garcia's on the phone trying to get an update."

"What's up with the bodies?"

"Four males. GSWs. This looks like it just happened. Call me and let me know what you get out there. Get some backup and get inside that building. I'm going to make the call to get people inside the other two places that we already stopped at as well."

"Okay. I'll get you an update when we get one," Steve said.

"Talk soon." I ended the call and immediately started dialing. We needed officers in the other businesses, we needed a forensics team in the building that we were in, and we needed to find that damned van.

CHAPTER 24

I clicked off from my call with Steve and slid my phone into my pocket. The property Steve and Ryan were at was empty, and they were just beginning to look around inside. He said he'd call me with any updates. We were still waiting on search warrants to get into the Carol City and Miramar locations.

"How did you guys see inside the building?" Buckley asked. With Colt and Gomez handling the scene in Miami Gardens, Buckley and Craig Town, from the forensics night shift, had been called in to give us a hand. They'd been on scene a few minutes.

"Garcia went around the building and saw the bullet holes ripped through the back wall. He said he put his eye to one and saw that body on the ground behind the vans."

Buckley turned around and got a look. With nothing other than the metal itself making up the exterior wall, we could see daylight coming in from a pair of quarter-sized holes in the building.

"Guessing our shooter or shooters were somewhere in that direction," I said and pointed. "Probably where those casings are by the door leading into the front of the store. Seems like we can probably use the locations of the spent casings to see where the shots came from."

Buckley nodded and snapped another photo of the deceased man in the back of the van. He let his camera hang. "We'll get them all marked and collected. On a different note, there was something in the back of this van," he said.

I took a few steps to have a look as he pointed inside.

"The guy's body is kind of out of the position that I believe it would've been in, plus we have some voids in the blood. See those two areas there?" he asked.

I did. To the right of the deceased man was an odd-shaped three-foot void free of any blood spatter that the rest of the van was covered in.

"I wouldn't mind getting this van back to the lab to be processed after we're through here," Buckley said.

"It's going to be a tight fit," I said. "I think Colt will probably have a few vehicles going back to the garages as well."

"If we have to take them to the Eighty-Second Street garages, we will."

The garages were about a half mile from our station. The facility was basically a county storage complex consisting of six huge pole sheds behind fence and barbed wire. Our SWAT vans, armored vehicles, and the rest of the county's toys were housed there. Along with the SWAT fleet and storage, one of the buildings was outfitted with a line of vehicle lifts. A full-time crew of mechanics worked there and kept busy with repairs and maintenance on the county's cruisers.

"What did we get from the cameras?" Buckley asked.

"I'm waiting on Wade to get here, but from what I can tell, we have a missing hard drive. There's a ball of wires next to a monitor off to the side in one of the offices. I followed a couple of the wires, which lead to a camera."

"So probably a bust?" he asked.

"We'll see. Anything standing out at you with the bodies?"

"These guys were all double tapped," Buckley said.

"The double tap matches the scene that Colt and Gomez are on. A pair of bodies there showed signs of the same."

"So, could be the same shooter?"

"Or just someone making sure nothing was left to chance," I said. I thought about the Camry that Steve said was at the other carpet-cleaning location. The car needed to be processed and its tags run if they hadn't been already. I fired off a text to Steve, looking for answers. A moment later, I received a response that Colt was sending someone out to start processing the scene. I asked about the tags on the Camry. Steve said they came back registered to the carpet-cleaning business and he'd made the call to the station to get someone looking into who owned the business itself.

"Give me a shout if you need or find anything, Buckley. I'm going outside to see if I can get an update from the locals."

"You got it," he said.

I headed from the garage door void into the parking lot. Most of the spots had been filled with patrol cars. Sergeant Foster, a mid-forties woman with blond hair in a ponytail and wearing black sunglasses, was our lead on scene. I found her talking with some other officers at her cruiser.

"Sergeant," I said. "What did we come up with?" The last I'd heard, officers had been talking with the neighboring businesses and asking questions about the goings-on at the store. The two officers dispersed when I walked up.

"Can't say we got a ton to work with," she said. "The consensus from the pizza place and that tire store there was that this place was exactly what it said it was. No one mentioned ever seeing anything amiss."

"Does either of the neighboring businesses have cameras that catch this place?" I asked.

She shook her head. "Both have cameras that face their parking lots. Except one parking lot faces the street, and the other faces away. And before you ask, the one that faces the street has a camera that doesn't catch the street, so no luck there."

"Great," I said. "And I don't suppose anyone heard the gunshots over here either?"

She shook her head but said nothing.

"So, we have two neighboring businesses operated by and frequented by nothing but deaf and blind people?" I asked. "I mean, seriously, how does someone fire off twenty rounds or so in the middle of the day in this setting and no one hear it?"

"Suppressed, maybe," she said.

That was really the only thing that made sense, but it still didn't tell me how no one could have seen a thing.

"And think about it," she continued, "how much attention would you give this place?"

She had a point. I imagined a carpet-cleaning business wouldn't get a second glance from anyone passing by or working next door. That was probably the reason the business was selected for moving drugs.

I did my best to bury my annoyance, hoping we'd get more from the other locations. "Any news on the van?"

"We put the description out to all the neighboring precincts but haven't heard anything," she said.

I shook my head. Ten minutes had passed before we had a helicopter overhead and searching the area for the van. It seemed ten minutes was the exact amount of time it took for whoever was driving it to disappear off the face of the earth. My phone rang, and I excused myself from the sergeant to take the call.

"Yeah, Tillerson," I answered.

"I just saw your message," he said. "I have some people looking into those names. I haven't got anything back, though."

The last text that I'd sent him was with the IDs of the dead men at the previous scene. Through everything that had been happening, I hadn't gotten around to sending him a message or calling him with the latest information on the carpet-cleaning businesses and the current scene.

"When you get something there, you can fill me in," I said. "I've got another handful of names for you, and we've had some developments."

"Developments like what?" he asked.

"More bodies." I filled Tillerson in on the scene, the van smashing from the garage and disappearing, and the names

165

that the vehicles in the parking lots came back registered to. Tillerson mentioned being familiar with a couple of them—mainly Rosanna Kimmel. He said she was a familiar face as far as street pushers. He was going to look into the rest of the names and let me know what he found out. I told him that we were going to need a meeting with everyone as soon as we all got back. There was too much going on, too many different scenes, and too many questions. I wanted all hands on deck so we could collectively come up with a plan. We set a time of six thirty at the station. I'd put the word out to everyone else the moment I had a chance. I ended my call with Tillerson and didn't get my phone back into my pocket before it rang again—Steve.

"Yeah," I answered.

"We've got a mess over here," he said.

"Now what?" I asked.

"I just had a good look at a drug lab and three dead bodies."

I needed clarification on about every word that had come from Steve's mouth. I'd just talked to him, and he'd said they got in and cleared the place. What he didn't mention on the call was a drug lab and bodies. "What?" I asked.

"Drug lab through a secret doorway. Inside were three DBs."

"Let's hear it start to finish," I said.

"This place looked as if it was laid out like the others, with the office in front and a warehouse in the back. We got inside and cleared it like I told you. We found nothing on our first sweep. After I talked to you, I went in and had a better look around. We started smelling gasoline in the warehouse area, yet we couldn't really find the source. Ryan said it was strongest in one of the offices, so we get in there and start poking around. We find half of a bloody footprint under a damned bookcase on the wall. Turns out, the bookcase is actually a door. Leads into a—"

"Hidden lab," I said.

"Yeah, and this place isn't of the 'meth heads cooking crank in their garage' variety. This looks like a professional operation here. All stainless and glass equipment. What looks to be a commercial ventilation system. Some big weird-looking machine in the back corner. High-dollar stuff. All three of our bodies are in lab coats. Looks like none of them were armed."

"Shell casings?" I asked.

"All over."

"Caliber?"

I heard Steve ask Ryan if he got a good look at the casings. I didn't catch Ryan's response.

"We didn't get a look at them," Steve said. "We only stayed in the room for a moment. We confirmed the men as deceased and exited. There's a gasoline barrel in there with a bullet hole through it that looks like it leaked a bunch of gasoline onto the floor. With all the chemicals and fuel in there, it's not someplace we want to be until someone gives us the okay. We'll probably have to get the fire department or someone out here."

"All right," I said. I filled Steve in on the plans for a meeting, told him to give me an update when he had one, and ended the call. I dug my fingers into my eyes. Our body count was rising rapidly. I imagined the media was going to be all over the case by the end of the night. I needed some damn answers and didn't have a clue where to find them.

CHAPTER 25

Frank

"Where are you?" Matt asked.

"In the garage of some house," Frank said. "I'm pulling the vinyl wrap off the van. As soon as it's all off, I'll head back to the house. I haven't heard the helicopter in a good half hour. I think they called it off."

"Back the hell up. Tell me how exactly you have the van in someone's garage."

"I needed to get off the damn street, and there was an open garage, so I pulled in."

"And that's it? Just an open garage waiting for you to hide out in. What a miracle."

Frank could hear the annoyance and sarcasm in his brother's words. "Look, I made a couple turns and found myself in a residential area. There was an open garage door. An older woman was working in her yard. I pulled into her garage."

"While she was in the yard? And she, what, just thought it was no big deal that you pulled into her garage?"

"She came to the garage wondering what the hell was going on, and I put a gun on her. Told her to get inside the house and then closed the garage door."

"And the woman? She's just inside watching TV while you use her garage?"

Frank didn't respond.

"Hello?" Matt said.

"She's tied up. I didn't hurt her. Someone will find her after I'm long gone," Frank said. The first two statements were lies. The third would probably end up being true.

"And you're sure these cops didn't see you?" Matt asked.

"Positive."

"Let me hear how it went down again."

"I'd pulled the van I drove into the building to get the money loaded up after I took care of everyone. Just as I finished, I heard banging on the front glass. I went to the cameras and saw the two cops outside. The door was locked, so I figured I'd just hang tight. Well, I watch them head for the garage doors, so I go over there to have a listen. I can hear them talking. At first it sounded like the one guy was on the phone. He mentioned the Camry at the Hialeah Gardens store, and it sounded like the police or someone was there. The guys sounded like they were about to leave, then the one says he heard something inside. I don't know what the hell he heard, because I wasn't moving. Then the other tells him to try to get a look around back. The next thing I know, the one guy is yelling that he saw a body inside. How he saw in, I don't know. There's no windows out back. Either way, they were going to call in backup or come inside. I had to act. I jumped in the van and blasted through the door. I made sure I took out their car and hit it up the block."

"So, they have the lab?" Matt asked.

"If they find it inside the building. But yeah, it sounded like they were there."

"They'll find it. How far are you away from the Gladeview store right now?"

"Maybe a half mile," Frank said.

"One- or two-car garage?" Matt asked.

"Two."

"And it was empty?"

"Yeah. I think her car was parked on the street or something. There's some boxes and other junk in here. Only one car would fit inside."

"Did you ask if this woman lived alone?" Matt asked. "Or are you about to get surprised by a husband?"

"Don't know, didn't ask. I'm only going to be here for another couple minutes."

"Whatever," Matt said. "So aside from the police bullshit, did you get everything done?"

"All the stores are closed. All employees have been terminated. Drugs and cash are in the van. We're good."

"All right. Good. Just get your ass back here with the van and everything inside of it. Tomorrow we'll be feet up on a beach, drink in hand."

"Looking forward to it. See you in a bit."

Frank ended the call and jumped into the driver's seat of the van. He pushed the van's airbag back at the steering wheel. The last of the van's vinyl graphics were on the hood, and he'd need to back up a foot or so to have enough room to take them off. Frank fired the engine and stared out the windshield. The woman who owned the home was pinned between the nose of the van and the back wall of the garage. She'd been sweeping the garage floor when he'd pulled in. Frank had expected to just run her over, but she'd clung to the front of his van. He slammed her into the back wall while doing at least ten miles an hour. She moaned for the first five minutes or so but had been dead quiet for over a half hour. Her arms lay lifeless on the van's hood. Her mouth was open and had spilled blood over the hood's center logo. Her crushed body fell from view when Frank backed up.

CHAPTER 26

We left the scene in Gladeview around five thirty and fought the evening rush hour traffic for the ten miles to Hialeah Gardens. In a roundabout way, the location was on our way back to the station, and I wanted to personally lay eyes on the scene and lab. Halloway had called to let me know that we'd secured warrants for the Miramar and Carol City locations. He said he'd keep me updated with whatever developed there.

Around six, Garcia and I pulled into the industrial area where the Hialeah Gardens carpet-cleaning business was located. Huge metal buildings with garage doors and loading docks lined the street we drove in on. Semi trailers and cars were scattered about the road's edges. We rounded a bend in the road and found more of the same for over a quarter mile. The road came to a T ahead.

"Make a left, and this place is going to be on our right. Looks like the first street after the turn."

"Got it," I said.

I followed Garcia's directions and made the first turn. The street we wanted came up within a few hundred feet. I made the turn down the dead-end street. Behind a fence to our left, industrial cranes poked up into the sky. To our right was the back of a giant building. Directly ahead, the street ended in front of some railroad tracks.

"This is us on the left up here," Garcia said.

I didn't need his directions. Five or six marked police cruisers, two fire trucks, Colt's pickup truck, and a coroner's van were parked around a standalone square building. As I turned in to the lot, I spotted the gold Camry parked off to the side of the business's front doors. We parked and went to the open front door of the place. I told a pair of local officers who appeared to be manning the doorway who we were and entered the building. As we walked in, I noticed a camera positioned to catch whoever was at the front door. The showroom of the place didn't look much different from the carpet-cleaning store we'd just left. The show floor held some chemicals, carpet-cleaning machines for rental, a front desk, and two offices. On the front desk was a full-face respirator with an evidence marker beside it.

I spotted the hall that led past the front desk, and Garcia and I took it toward the rear warehouse. As with the location we'd just come from, a metal security door separated the front of the business from the back. I imagined it had been left open since it looked like a code was required for entry. We passed through into the warehouse.

Immediately inside were two vans facing an open garage door to my right. On the walls next to the vans were shelves with cleaning equipment and supplies. There were no bodies, and nothing looked amiss. To our left were three offices where everyone seemed to be gathered. Some uniformed officers spoke to Gomez. I got a nod from Ryan, who was talking to Skip near the front door of the last office. Through the glass window, I could see the doorway, which I figured led to the lab inside. We headed over.

"Hey," Ryan said.

"What's up, guys," I said.

"What's up is that the county is going to have to add another wing to my office if this keeps up," Skip said. He leaned against the wall with his arms crossed over his big belly. Skip wore a light-blue long-sleeved button-up shirt and matching latex gloves. A black lanyard with the word "Coroner" in yellow hung around his neck, holding his credentials. "To say that we're going to be swamped with this for a few days is putting it lightly," Skip added.

"Just get us what you can when you can, Skip," I said. "We're going to do whatever the hell we can to make sure you don't get any more."

"It would be appreciated," he said.

I caught a camera mounted toward the top of the wall above the offices. It was aimed straight down at us. "Any luck on the cameras?".

"Either the hard drive is gone," Ryan said, "or they were just for show. All the wires go back to a monitor in that first office but aren't plugged into anything."

"Basically, the same as what we found at the last place," Garcia said.

"Any computers anywhere?" I asked. I'd noticed at the last location that there wasn't a computer or phone aside from one at the front desk. And Wade had confirmed that the computer was of the point-of-sale variety only. It didn't have internet capability, but Wade took it, anyway.

"Nothing but the front desk. One phone, one computer," Ryan said.

"All right. We'll get Wade out for the computer," I said. "At the last place, the front desk one was just a point-of-sale system. Maybe we'll have better luck with this one." I pointed into the office. "This is our secret entrance?"

"Yeah," Ryan said. He motioned for Garcia and me to follow and entered the office. "Steve and Colt are inside. The fire department guys just gave us the okay to get in there about twenty minutes ago."

"All right. Anything since we last talked?" I asked.

"Not really," Ryan said. "As soon as Colt is done with all the photos of the bodies in there, we'll get them out and see what we can do about getting some IDs on the guys."

"Okay," I said.

Ryan had stopped at the open doorway. He pointed down. "There's our bloody footprint, so watch that," he said.

"Got it," I said.

"But check this thing out," Ryan said. He grabbed the big white bookcase and swung it toward us until it clicked and closed.

I took a step back and had a look. The bookcase was covered in fingerprint powder, and the shelves held photographs and plaques. Some fake plants, books, and random knickknacks completed the look. Unless someone knew, no one would be able to tell that the bookcase was a doorway.

"This stuff is all glued down so it doesn't move when the door opens and closes," Ryan said. "The other offices have similar bookcases, but they don't open. Honestly, I don't think we would have found this if it hadn't been for the print." He pointed at it, and only the toe half was visible under the closed bookshelf doorway. Ryan reached up with his gloved hand and pulled something that released the door. "We already printed the whole bookshelf area," he said. "This has a latch up here like a pair of double entry doors does where a pin extends into a slot." Ryan pulled the door open. "After you."

I walked into a cinder block–walled room about twenty feet by thirty. A body lay on the ground just a few feet from the doorway. The man appeared to have taken a bullet to the head and another pair center mass—it was becoming a recurring trait in the investigation. Stainless steel vats lined the walls, and some were on stands. Tubing ran from container to container. Fifty-gallon drums of fuel wrapped in cellophane stood in the corner near bottles of what looked like iodine. Cardboard boxes filled with chemicals stood on a rack wall behind them. A big stainless steel cylindrical machine with a yellowed glass container attached to the front took up another corner of the room. Colt and Steve stood near an overturned table, where Colt photographed a dead man at their feet. I spotted another body to the guy's right. Each downed man wore a lab coat and gloves.

"Looks like our shooter or shooters from the old horse track are having a busy day," Colt said.

"Double taps on each guy?" I asked.

"Looking like it. Same caliber casings. When you add the car out front, I'm saying we have a pretty good chance at it being connected."

"Guess they went from one place to the next," I said.

"It looks like it," Steve said. He took his eyes from the man at his feet and looked up at me. "Hell of a little secret lab, huh?"

"Yeah," I said. "We need to know who the hell owns these carpet-cleaning businesses. Or who was paying the lease if the buildings weren't owned by the business."

"We have to dig into it," Ryan said. "The word that came back from records was some kind of trust owned the properties. I'm guessing we know how that's going to go. The trust will belong to some corporation or holding company. A bunch of running around and we'll never find the single person behind everything."

"There has to be someone somewhere writing the checks to keep the lights on here. Let's find out who it is and get them answering questions."

Ryan nodded.

"Anything, Colt?" I asked.

"What you see is what we have. Three DBs. GSWs. Casings are from a forty-five. We'll print every last thing in here and find out where the hell everything came from. A lot of this stuff looks commercial in nature. We'll get the brand and see if we can hunt down anything there. I imagine we can get something from that dryer. That's not everyday equipment anywhere other than a chemical lab."

"Dryer?" I asked.

Colt poked his chin toward the corner, at the big machine with the glass tube attached. "That's a spray dryer. Basically, it turns a liquid to a powder using hot air. A liquid product, whatever that may be, sprays down from a needle in the top of that glass container. Hot air dries the product and feeds it through a tube into a catch bag at the end of that tube there."

"That looks to me like something too fancy to be used for cooking Krokodil," I said.

"It is. I mean if this is being made the same way as, say, cocaine or heroin, usually they just brick up some paste and microwave it. Someone is taking pride in their product," Colt said. "Or was, I should say."

Ryan twirled his finger in a circle in the air. "Everything to make drugs but no drugs," he said.

"Maybe whoever did this left with them," Garcia said.

I nodded my head toward the front of the building. "Anything with the Toyota outside?" I asked.

"We gave it a quick look, but that was about it," Steve said.

"We haven't processed it yet," Colt said. "Gomez was just about to get on it, though."

Steve let out a big breath. "So, what the hell is this? What the hell are we in the middle of?"

"I don't know," I said. "And we're not getting a ton of help from Tillerson or his people on the streets. Doesn't seem like anyone knows a damn thing."

"This has to be some kind of takeover," Steve said. "Cartel, maybe."

"Seems too clean," I said. "Too neat."

"Neat or not, I'm going with rival drug organization of some sort," Garcia said.

"What about the DEA?" Ryan asked. "Maybe it's time we picked up the phone on this."

"I was kicking it around on the way over here," I said. "And we're going to have to call them. Especially after finding this lab."

My cell phone vibrated against my leg. I pulled it out to see Halloway calling.

"Yeah, Cap," I answered.

"We've got three more bodies at the Carol City location," he said.

"You've got to be shitting me."

"I haven't gotten word back on the Miramar store yet," he said.

CHAPTER 27

I'd gotten a handful of texts from Amy and my mother asking when I'd be home. The only thing I could respond with was to not wait up. Garcia and I drove north and met with the local PD at the Carol City store—I wanted to lay eyes on the scene myself. It was almost identical to the others. The layout of the building was the same as the Gladeview store. Three men had been gunned down in the warehouse. Forty-five-caliber shell casings were strewn across the floor.

The local officers questioned every neighboring business— no one had heard a sound. No one had seen anything questionable. We weren't on the scene in Carol City more than ten minutes when we got the call that we had more bodies at the Miramar location. We made the trip a few miles farther north to Miramar. When we got there, it was simply more of the same, with four bodies instead of three. We didn't get back to the station and started with our meeting until almost eight o'clock.

I closed the door of the conference room and walked to my seat at the filled table. Dave and his night shift guys sat with

Steve, Ryan, and Garcia. Halloway took up a spot to my right. Colt, Gomez, Buckley, and Town held down the side of the table nearest the glass looking out over the bull pen. Tillerson, wearing street clothes, lingered around the coffee station next to Wade. We had too many names and too many bodies. Sorting through just whatever the hell it was that we were investigating was going to be an investigation in itself.

"What's our total?" Halloway asked.

"Nineteen today," I said. "Twenty-one when you add Frost and Nance."

"Nineteen bodies today," Halloway said.

"Yeah." I dug my index finger and thumb into my eyes. "We'd found another seven bodies between the carpet-cleaning businesses in Miramar and Carol City. That was added to the seven bodies at the Hialeah Gardens and Gladeview locations. We had five at the overgrown horse track facility. And that's what we know about."

"Okay. So, nineteen bodies," the captain said. "And who are our suspects?"

The room went silent.

"Witnesses to one of the nineteen homicides?" Halloway asked. "Where are we with them? Let me hear some names."

Again, he didn't get a response.

I knew what Halloway was doing, and the captain had done it in the past when we had next to nothing on an investigation. He'd give us an ass chewing so he could pass on that he did so when the chief and major came chewing ass on him. I figured after another question or two, he'd decide his point had been made and we could get back to the meeting.

"So how are we looking on leads? Who is doing what?" Halloway asked. The captain crossed his arms over his belly and leaned back in his chair as his line of sight moved around the table.

Colt looked like he was about to say something, but I gave him a quick headshake. Anything he said at that moment would provoke an attack from the captain.

"Don't all talk at once," Halloway said. He held his hands up like he wanted a response.

No one uttered a word.

"Twenty-one bodies and we don't have a damned thing," the captain said. "Two of those were fellow officers. Not a witness, not a lead, not a suspect, not a clue. Tell me how I present that to the major and chief?"

I figured I'd take a bullet for the team if one was coming. "Cap, we had nineteen bodies dumped on us in a day. Some of our leads were those bodies. We have all the forensics to sort through. We have this business to dig into. We have fifteen positive identities of the deceased. We need to positively ID the rest and look into each person individually. We'll find something, but we need the time to do so."

His head snapped toward me, but he didn't speak. He looked like he was grinding his teeth, but I think I gave him too much logic to counter. Halloway sniffed, cracked his neck, and turned his head toward Tillerson. "You've got to tell us something."

"I've got every person who works in my department trying to find out what the hell is going on," Tillerson said. "We're pressing on every contact, every CI and snitch that we know of."

"And?" Halloway asked.

"Whatever is going down isn't something that anyone knows about. This Krokodil thing itself was real hush-hush to begin with. Nobody really knew where the stuff was coming from or who was pumping it out on the streets. We got that Frost and Nance had been talking with the Tavaras guy about a meeting with someone, but that's all the file said. And Tavaras is dead, so we can't squeeze him."

"What about Tavaras's crew?" Steve asked. "Do we know who they are? Can we lean on any of them? Maybe they know who Tavaras had been talking to."

"Already trying to hunt down a couple of known associates of his," Tillerson said.

"What about your contact that you reached out to?" I asked. "Did he know Lattore's name? Maybe he knows something about what went down today."

"I haven't heard from him yet," Tillerson said.

"Who are you talking about?" Halloway asked.

Tillerson had taken a seat on the table beside the coffeemaker. "His name is Mullin," he said. "He was a UC for us a few years ago. He's been working with the feds since."

"And he knows what?" Halloway asked.

"I just reached out to him to see if he'd heard anything or knew Lattore's name," Tillerson said. "I'll ask him if he heard anything about today when I talk to him. Keep in mind, this guy is a UC for the feds, and his calling me is a courtesy because he used to work for us. If it's not safe for him to call, he won't call."

Halloway nodded.

"We're going to have to bring the DEA in on this," I said. "I don't know who else, but I'm sure they'd be real interested in that lab. Who knows, maybe they've seen something similar before, and it could point us in a direction."

Halloway nodded. "Do we have photos of everything from today?"

"Being developed as we speak. Probably a few hundred," Colt said. "Every scene, every body, a good amount from the lab we found, down to individual pieces of equipment."

"What all do you guys have working down there?" Halloway asked.

"Prints to process that were lifted from the bodies. Prints to process from each location. Hundreds of them, and we could probably go back and lift hundreds more. Besides the prints, we have a total of eleven vehicles to process, including the carpet-cleaning vans. And the vans will all have to go to one of our storage garages to be gone over. We don't have room for them here. Then there are the vehicles that were parked at the carpet-cleaning businesses and belonged to some of our deceased. We'll have to leave them in the tow company's lot until we can find a place to take them and we have the manpower to process them."

"Did we get anything from Frost's Mercedes or Nance's SUV?" Steve asked.

Colt shook his head.

"What else?" Halloway asked.

"All the ballistics evidence whenever Skip gets all the bullets removed and sent to us. Going through each photo we took, writing reports on it all. Possibly checking into each victim's home. We literally got a month or two of work dumped on us in a matter of a few hours."

"Work the prints, then whatever you feel is the next most important thing in line," the captain said. "Whatever you feel is going to give us our best chance at a lead."

Colt nodded. "I've got all hands on deck. The prints are being entered into the system as we speak."

"Video evidence? Cell phones? Computers? What are our tech guys working on?" The captain's eyes moved to Wade.

"Each of these businesses was basically set up the same, a single landline and a POS system at the front counter. The credit cards ran through the point-of-sale system. Nothing else. Not one of the offices in the back had a phone or computer. There was no router for Wi-Fi. Each place had a similar security system setup, and the hard drive was removed from each."

"Phones on the deceased?" Halloway asked.

"Not a single one on any of the bodies from the carpet-cleaning stores," I said. "Either taken from the dead men or they simply weren't allowed to have them inside the building."

"The hope is that we can get some from the vehicles outside in the parking lots," Wade said. "Either that or we'll have to locate the numbers for the deceased through family and try to get ahold of records that way."

"What about phones on the guys from the old horse track?" Halloway asked.

"None found," I said.

The captain shook his head. "All right. You said we have fifteen positive IDs to work?"

"Yeah," I said. "I have the list of names in my office but

haven't put anything together with all of their sheets yet."

"What time do we have?" Halloway asked. He squinted as he looked at the clock on the wall, which showed a bit after eight thirty. "Let's get started on those names. Pull the sheets and get them written up on the board. I'm going to parade everyone in the building and everyone over in the patrol building past it. Finding out who is responsible for these deaths is now job number one. For everyone. And someone find me who the hell owns these damned businesses."

CHAPTER 28

Frank

Frank pulled the van into the big garage, parked next to a dust-covered Lamborghini, and killed the engine. He stepped out and went to the van's back doors. Each bag of money was removed and stacked off to the side.

He left the garage and walked to the house. Frank could smell something cooking the second he entered. He found Matt in the kitchen, tending to a frying pan on the stove.

"Good timing. Food is almost done," Matt said.

"What did you make?"

"Mom's chicken Madeira. Are we good?"

"Yeah, we're all set," Frank said. He tossed the keys for the van onto the big granite-topped kitchen island. "The van is parked in the garage. I stacked the bags of money in front of it. When is Jorge coming for the pickup?"

"I just talked to him an hour or so ago. He said he was going to send someone over in the morning to pick it up. They made fifty?"

"That's what it looked like, yeah."

"Well, is it or isn't it? The deal was for fifty kilos. It needs to be fifty."

"I'll double-check. It's probably more."

"More is fine, less is not."

"I'll go back out there and get an exact count in a minute," Frank said. "So, the fifty covers everything Jorge is doing for us?"

"Yup."

"Cool. What do we need to do yet?"

"Get all the money and whatever we're taking with us loaded into the big boat," Matt said. "After that, we wrap up some last-minute details and then leave tomorrow afternoon."

"Roger brought the boat?"

Matt rocked his head back and forth and tapped a wooden spoon on the side of the pan before him. "He didn't personally. Two of his guys showed up with it a few hours ago. The boat is docked down at the water. The guys are in the shed."

"Dead?"

"Yeah," Matt said.

"What's the plan for Roger?" Frank asked.

"He's one of the details that needs to be wrapped up. We'll take a trip to the marina later tonight to deal with him."

"What about his guys?" Frank asked.

"They're not going anywhere."

"I know. I mean won't Roger be looking for them? Obviously, he knows that they were bringing the boat here."

"Well, he isn't going to come here looking for them. And if he calls looking for them, I'll just say that I asked them to hang out and party. What the hell can he say to that?"

"All right. How are we looking with everything else?"

"Everything for the trip down south is set. We're supposed to meet a friend of Jorge's at a little marina in Marathon tomorrow evening. That guy is going to transfer all our things to another boat, and we'll push off for Cuba. Jorge said he was going to pick us up personally and take us to the new house."

"And the house is ready?" Frank asked.

"As ready as it's going to be," Matt said. "We should be good."

"Good as long as the feds don't catch up to us," Frank said.

"That isn't going to be something that we have to worry about. The feds haven't even tried to contact me for weeks. If someone did eventually catch our trail, it'll be gone next month when we jump again. They'll be chasing ghosts."

"What about Vice? They've been calling," Frank said.

"Vice doesn't have anything. Their investigation died with Frost and Nance. I know the guy who has been calling. His name is Tillerson. He was a sergeant when I was in Vice. Aside from tipping me off about Paul, it sounds like he's just fishing for information. I wouldn't worry that they're going to break whatever case they're working by tomorrow afternoon and show up on our doorstep."

"Yeah," Frank said. "Probably not. Oh, hey, did our new IDs come?"

"Yup. All our paperwork is set. It's in my office. New everything—name, bank account, social, credit cards, insurance, everything. You're going to cease being Frank Mullin and start being whoever the hell the new name is. At least until we make our second jump into South America and you get another name."

"Damn, we're really doing it, huh?" Frank said.

"That was the deal. The first sniff we got of someone investigating, everyone goes, the business is done, and we're out of the country. No screwing around."

Frank nodded. "What's my new name?"

"I don't know. I think it was something Varela. Diego, maybe."

"Diego Varela?" Frank asked. "Do I look like a Diego to you?"

"No, to me you look like my brother, Frank. To anyone else that you meet from here forward, you'll look like whatever the hell name is on that paperwork."

Frank looked dissatisfied. "What's the new name you got?"

"I think it was Gabriel Perez or something." Matt shredded some cheese across a grater into the pan before him.

"So, we're not brothers anymore?" Frank asked.

"You expected Jorge to find us related aliases that were going to check out?" Holding a big ball of mozzarella in hand, Matt looked over at Frank.

Frank shrugged. "Where are we supposed to be from? Because we don't look especially Hispanic."

"Spain, Argentina, wherever. Make something up. Or better yet, don't tell anyone shit. That will work too." Matt went back to cooking.

"We don't speak—"

"Quit worrying about it," Matt said. "It'll be fine. You'll adjust. We'll hire someone to tutor you for a few weeks. I'll make sure she's hot."

"Fine," Frank said. "What time did you want to go out by Roger?"

"Later." Matt clicked off the burner beneath the pan, removed it from the range top, and placed the entire pan in the oven. He went to the refrigerator and pulled out two bottles of beer. Matt twisted the tops off both bottles and took a seat at the kitchen island. "Food will be done in five. Sit. Chill out." Matt slid a beer toward Frank. He leaned his bottle neck out toward his brother.

Frank tapped it. "Cheers."

"Enjoy your last day being an American," Matt said.

Frank took a drink, pulled off his guns, and draped them over the back of a chair beside him.

CHAPTER 29

I didn't get home until damn near ten o'clock. I'd sent a text to Amy right before we started the meeting. She and my parents were on their way to dinner at the Italian place she and I often went to up the street from the house. Amy offered to order for me on the chance that I could make it to meet them. I didn't. When I got home, my skirt steak in a mushroom wine sauce sat in a Styrofoam container in my refrigerator waiting for me. I ate, had a beer with my father, and went straight to bed.

Up by six and back to work by seven, I arrived to the news that Dave was interviewing someone at the patrol station out front. I grabbed a doughnut and a coffee from the lunchroom and walked next door. Chestnut was seated at the desk that faced the window into the interview room. His blond hair had been shaggy as of late—he'd mentioned something about his missus wanting him to try a new look. Officer Nate Lucerne, a mid-thirties patrolman, stood looking over Chestnut's shoulder in the observation room. I imagined Lucerne, who I'd seen doing office duty several times, had given room access to Dave.

"Hey, morning," Chestnut said.

"Lieutenant," Lucerne said.

"What's up," I said.

Chestnut pointed at the interview room.

Through the glass, I saw Dave seated across from a bald-headed guy who had an entire face and scalp full of tattoos. He couldn't have been much older than his mid-twenties. I was betting that sometime in the next twenty years, he'd regret having the word "Hustle"—with a dollar sign for the s—tattooed across his forehead.

"I'll leave you guys to it. I hear a bear claw in the lunchroom calling my name," Lucerne said. He left the room.

"Who's this joker?" I asked and pointed my chin at the man being interviewed.

"Someone that Tillerson's guys dumped off," Chestnut said. "Antonio Javier Fernandez. Guess he is, or should I say was, part of this Tavaras guy's crew."

"What's he saying?" I asked.

"Nothing that I care to repeat. He hasn't asked for counsel but isn't exactly being forthcoming," Chestnut said.

"But he hasn't given us anything that can help," I said.

"Nope."

"Do we have a sheet on him?" I asked.

"Yeah, here." Chestnut scooped a few pieces of paper from the desk in front of him and held them out toward me. The list of priors seemed standard fare for a drug dealer—multiple charges of possession of marijuana, one distribution of narcotics, two unlawful possessions of controlled dangerous substances, one second-degree assault, two parole violations, and a pair of charges for possession of a controlled substance with intent to distribute.

Dave stood and exited the room, then he walked into our observation room a second later.

"Hey. Morning, Harrington," he said.

"Morning," I said. "Having any luck?"

"I'm learning new and creative things to call police officers," Dave said. "Quite a few different uses of the word 'pig.' Lots of four-letter words, and that would be in both English and Spanish."

"Always good to expand your vocabulary," I said. "What did this guy get brought in on, or how exactly did he come to be sitting here?"

"I guess some of Tillerson's vice guys pegged him as being associated with Tavaras. They went to shake his tree and caught him mid-deal. He had an ounce of what was figured to be Krokodil on him. Packaged for sale. Arrested him and dropped him on our doorstep. Tillerson said to call him when we finished with the guy."

I sat on the edge of the desk and crossed my arms over my chest. "Krokodil, huh. So good chance he could know something."

"Could be," Dave said.

"What did you ask him?"

"What he could tell me about Tavaras and who Tavaras had been dealing with regarding Krokodil. Where he got the Krokodil to sell. I implied that we could make this latest thing disappear for a little information. He responded by telling me to go away. Yet the first word was four letters and the second was 'off.'"

I turned my head to look at the guy seated at the room's metal table. I didn't know if it was the tattoos covering his face or what, but something told me that he simply wasn't going to talk no matter what we offered him.

"You want a swing at him?" Dave asked.

"Maybe in a second. Let's let him simmer for a minute. Did we get anything overnight?"

"We got that an offshore holding company out of Antigua owns the carpet-cleaning businesses. The number listed for the place is disconnected. The address is an empty lot when we look it up via satellite. We're going to have to look into the utilities, subpoena the power and phone company, and see who's paying the bills."

"I have my doubts it'll be that easy," I said.

"I would agree. Let's see, what did you miss? Not a lot, really. It's mostly just been Chestnut and me working it. We got a call around one o'clock. Female, forties, in a trailer park over by Coral Gables. GSW. I sent Malone and Burns out to it. The husband was on scene, intoxicated and claiming self-defense. Burns said the guy had a couple scuffs on him, so who knows. Neighbors say there had been domestic disputes in the past. Patrol confirmed that they'd been out to the location before. They brought the guy in and just wrapped up an hour or so ago."

Dave slid a chair next to Chestnut and plopped down. "As far as whatever the hell this drug thing is, up until this guy got dumped in our lap, we've been looking up each individual arrest that each of our victims had. Vice seems to know quite a few of these guys, and a couple of the guys I talked to over there say that our list of names reads like a who's who of local low-level drug dealers. My thinking was, check into their past arrests and see who they were busted with. Besides seeing which of these victims we can tie to each other, I wanted to see if we can find anyone busted with our vics that's still breathing."

"And?" I asked.

"It's not bearing much fruit. We got two guys. One, a guy by the name of Xavier Pelly, was busted on a drug charge with a Howard Portnow in the past. This Pelly seems like another low-level dealer. I say that because he's been locked up for the last six months for dealing. We can check jail records to see if these two had been in contact, but I doubt it's going to do much good. The other, a guy by the name of Davante Simpson, had a prior with a victim from the Gladeview location named Clint Turpin. The only problem there is Mr. Simpson is dead."

"Doesn't sound like much luck there," I said.

"Not really. Friends and family might be our best route for answers. I was going to have Burns and Malone start dialing after they got back, but we don't know who Skip has and hasn't talked to. I don't want one of my guys to get caught on the phone in a situation where the family doesn't know why a detective is calling, you know."

"Yeah," I said. "I'll call Skip and see who he's contacted. Anything new from Forensics?"

"They got us two more IDs on the victims from prints. That, and we got all the carpet-cleaning vans transported to the garages on Eighty-Second. The word was that someone from Forensics was going to be stationed over there today working on getting whatever we can from them."

"What about the cars in the lots of the carpet places?" I asked.

"Towed, but sitting at the tow lot until we have room," Dave said.

"Okay," I said. "So, no more bodies overnight, at least in regard to this case, but not a lot in the way of moving forward."

"About the gist of it," Dave said. "Unless this guy starts singing for some reason." He pointed through the glass. "Which I'm doubting."

"What exactly is this guy looking at?" I asked.

"Probably a little bit of a stretch," Chestnut said. "His priors aren't helping him any. A new dealing charge may land him an easy year or more."

"Let me go and say hi," I said. "You want to get back in there?"

"Run it solo. I don't think he likes me," Dave said.

I smirked, walked next door, and entered the interview room. Mr. Fernandez locked eyes on me. He didn't blink and continued his dead-eyed gaze as I sat across from him. "Mr. Fernandez, I'm Lieutenant Nash Harrington. I'd like to ask you a couple questions regarding your possession of Krokodil."

"I'm not telling you shit, pig." He followed up by telling me to go have relations with myself, though not quite that politely. As he spoke, I saw that he had top and bottom rows of silver teeth.

"That's great," I said. "Let me make this real short and sweet." I put my elbows up on the metal desk, clasped my hands together, and stared at my tattooed friend. "We want information on where the Krokodil you were selling came from. We also want information on Carlos Tavaras. For those two things, we'll help you out of this latest charge. If not, I would imagine you'll be spending some time inside. Could be a year, could be more. Who knows? That's up to the judge. A judge who is going to take your priors into consideration while sentencing."

Fernandez said nothing. He sniffed and continued to stare at me. I returned his stare, looking at his teardrop tattoos that came down from each eye—two on the left and three on the right. His eyebrows had been shaved off and replaced with the words "love" and "hate." The word "insane" was tattooed in script across his left cheek.

"I have more important things to do than sit in here and waste my morning playing games with you. Are you talking or just going to jail?"

Fernandez lifted his cuffed hands that were chained to the table and gave me a pair of middle fingers.

"Enjoy that cell, buddy," I said. I rose from the chair and left the room.

CHAPTER 30

Dave's team had passed off everything they'd been working on to us and headed home. Where Mr. Fernandez got sent off to, I didn't know—if he wasn't talking, we had no use for him. Halloway had been in a meeting with Mark Swanson, the Miami Police Department's PR guy, when I got back to my office after dealing with Fernandez. The pair had put together a press release, and Halloway went before the cameras just before ten o'clock. The statement said we'd had several related homicides that we believed involved the drug trade. It said that we would update the press as the investigation progressed. From what we'd talked about in the meeting the prior night, I'd thought we planned to give the press more.

Halloway called and asked me to his office. I headed over.

"What's up, Cap," I said.

"Sit," he said.

I pulled out a chair across from him at his desk.

"I didn't really get a chance to talk to you before we had to get in front of the cameras," he said. "We had to adjust what we wanted to say a bit."

"Yeah, I thought the thinking was to release a couple of the names to see what we got back."

"That was the plan until I talked to the DEA this morning. They wanted me to keep the information we released to a minimum."

"So, now they're in charge?"

"We've got two of our own involved in this with Frost and Nance, so they won't push us out, but I'm guessing that they'll be working with the bureau and who knows who else on it and essentially, yes, taking it over."

I figured as much but never liked it when we had to give up an investigation. Then I also knew why the captain was calling me into his office, to order me to put everything that we had in a nice little package to turn over to the DEA.

"If we're turning this over, what are we supposed to do with all of the evidence scattered all over? We've got who knows how many vehicles here and at the garages on Eighty-Second. We've got another who knows how many cars that were towed from the carpet-cleaning parking lots sitting in the tow lot, waiting to be started on. We've got Skip over at the ME's office with a cooler full of bodies. Some of those bodies have bullets in them that we need the ballistics run on. We've—"

Halloway held up his hand, cutting me off. "They're going to send someone or multiple someones over this afternoon. We can meet with them and develop a plan of action from there. I want you to get with Colt and Wade and get everything that we currently have written up put into a file, copied, or whatever."

"Yeah, I know the drill," I said. I rose from my chair and left the captain's office. After mumbling profanities under my breath as I took the elevator down, I went to the forensics department and found Colt in his office. He sat at his desk with his nose buried in some papers. I gave his door a tap and walked in.

"Hey," Colt said. He set the papers down and waved me in.

"Anything new?" I asked.

He tapped his fingertip on the photos he'd been looking at. "Just going over some stuff from the photos of the lab. Trying to put a list together of the equipment so we can start making calls and looking into recent orders. What's up?"

I shook my head. "I'm just popping in to give you a heads-up. Halloway wants us to put everything together for the DEA. Copies of everything," I said. "They'll be here to collect it this afternoon."

"How am I supposed to make copies of physical evidence that I'm in the middle of processing?" Colt asked.

"That's a good question," I said. "We'll have to figure out some way to transfer the evidence that's been collected."

"So, I should shut my guys down is what you're saying? I've got Gomez processing the vans out at the garages as we speak."

The thought of having everyone stop and do nothing while we waited for another agency to take over wasn't sitting right with me. I didn't care for the feeling and didn't plan to cease my work on the investigation until I was specifically told to do so. And it was probably going to take more than one person, and that person telling me more than one time, before I did. "You know what, Colt, you make the call. If you want your guys to continue working, let them. I'm going to keep doing what I was doing until someone stands in front of me and tells me not to. Once whoever gets here from the DEA, I'll deal with them."

"Looks like we're on the same page, then," Colt said.

"All right. Just giving you the heads-up. About to go down the hall and give the same to Wade."

Colt said nothing but gave me a nod. I left his office and the forensics department and walked to Wade in Tech. Like Colt, he was in his office at his desk. Wade saw me walk in, jammed half of what looked like a blueberry muffin in his mouth, and waved me over.

"Almost set with the subpoenas," Wade said. He spoke around a mouthful of half-chewed muffin. "Should hopefully be able to have phone records from the four carpet-cleaning stores by the end of the day. Then I need to find out all of our victims' phone carriers and try to get the paperwork together to get their phone records."

"All right. I was just in by Colt giving him the same information that I'm about to give you. You can do what you want with it."

"Um, okay," Wade said.

"This is getting turned over to the DEA this afternoon," I said. "It sounds like it'll be their baby after that. They'll want reports on what we've got so far."

"Well, then I guess they're going to get some blank sheets of paper. The phone companies are about the only thing we got going that I'm working on. The POS systems pulled from the places don't show us anything. I was planning on doing a little footwork with a few of my guys after we get the subpoenas set. Try to pound the pavement and find some video somewhere."

"Until the DEA is standing in front of me, I'm working the case. Colt sounded like he was doing the same."

"Looks like I'm with you guys, then," Wade said. "I'll get these subpoenas sent off, get my guys working with the others, and start ringing doorbells."

"Let me know what you get," I said.

"I will."

I left Wade in his office and walked upstairs. After a stop at the bull pen to let Steve, Ryan, and Garcia know the plans with the DEA, I headed to my office. The red light on my desk phone was flashing. I clicked the button to play the message. The automated voice said the message was one of two, and the first one played.

"Hi, Sweetie, it's your mom. I tried your cell phone, but you didn't answer. I left a message. I wanted to see if maybe you were interested in going to the casino on Sunday afternoon and playing bingo with your father and me. I think they said it started at three." I heard her ask my father if that was the right time, which he confirmed. "Yeah, three o'clock at the casino for bingo on Sunday. Amy sounded like she kind of wanted to go. Call me right away and let me know. Love you."

The recording stopped.

Why my mother needed to know right away about bingo

in two days, I didn't know. I'd give her a call when I got a chance. The second message started playing. It had come in a few minutes prior.

"Lieutenant, this is Paul D'Bruzzi. I just got a call in from my guys who say they may have spotted your boat. They're going to check in on it, and I'll give you a ring once I hear back from them."

The machine beeped, signaling the end of the recording. I dialed the marine unit.

"Sergeant D'Bruzzi."

"Hey, it's Harrington. I just got your message."

"Yeah, Lieutenant. I haven't heard anything back from my guys yet, but I'm guessing this could be your boat from what they said. Yellowfin 24 Bay, black upholstery and piping. It's in the water at Buck's Marina."

"Where is that?" I asked.

"Biscayne Boulevard and Northeast 135th Street, North Miami. It's back in the channels that lead out onto Biscayne Bay."

"Give me one second," I said. I pulled the place up on my computer. By road, the area was just a mile or so from where we'd found Frost and Nance's bodies. By water, Broad Causeway blocked a direct path, but I still didn't imagine the travel time was much more than twenty minutes. "This place is a stone's throw from where we found the boat on video."

"Yeah, it's right over there. Let me try to get my guys Wallace and Halep on the radio and see what they came up with. One minute."

I waited on the line while he made the call. Movement in

the bull pen caught my eye. Tillerson was walking to my office door. He leaned in my doorway.

"We've got a songbird," he said. "Damn, didn't see you were on the phone."

I took the receiver from my mouth. "I'm on hold. What's up?"

"This Fernandez guy is singing."

"Really?" I heard a click in my ear, and D'Bruzzi came back on. I held a finger up at Tillerson to give me a second.

"No answer at the place," D'Bruzzi said. "Pretty damn sure this is your boat, though. No registration numbers on it."

"All right. I'm going to send a couple people that way. Are your guys going to wait there?"

"They'll wait if you're sending people now."

"I am," I said.

"All right. I'll let them know."

"Appreciate the call," I said. "I owe you a beer."

"You know where our office is," he said.

I thanked him again and hung up.

"Something on the case?" Tillerson asked.

"Sounds like we found our boat. I'm going to send some of my guys out to sniff around. The marine unit is going to wait on it. Now what's going on with Fernandez? He didn't strike me as someone who was going to talk. Ever," I said.

"He didn't know Tavaras was dead," Tillerson said. "I went to have a chat with him. Pretty much the second I told him Tavaras had been tortured and killed, his words were 'I want a deal and I'll talk.'"

"Interesting," I said. "What does he want, and what is he offering for a deal?"

"It's already done. This latest arrest and charges to go along with it disappear in exchange for the person behind the Krokodil. He says he knows a name and where they live. I came to get you to go have a chat with him. He requested an attorney to look over the deal, so I think there's a public defender en route."

"He's still next door?" I asked.

"Still where you left him in the interview room."

"Okay. Let's head over there. I just need to stop at the bull pen quick to tell a couple of my guys to go meet the marine unit."

"Yup," Tillerson said.

I left my desk and followed him from my office.

CHAPTER 31

Matt

Matt had just gotten the front gate for Jorge's guy Javier. He and Frank went out front of the house and waited for the approaching silver Lexus sedan. A black cargo van followed the sedan up the driveway. The vehicles stopped at the fountain, and a man exited from each of the sedan's four doors. The men were all Hispanic, and all looked to be muscle for Jorge's operation—not one of the four was under two twenty-five. Three of the men remained near the door they'd exited. A big guy wearing a blue floral shirt and white pants left the front passenger door of the vehicle and headed toward Matt and Frank. No one emerged from the black van.

"One of you Matt?" the guy walking up asked.

Matt nodded. "Me."

"Javier," he said. "Jorge sent me."

The man held out his hand, and Matt shook it.

"Your goods are in there," Matt said. He motioned toward the garages.

"Can we get my van and guys inside to get loaded up?"

"That's fine," Matt said.

"All right. Let me go and let these guys know what's up."

"Sure," Matt said. He started walking to the garages, and Frank followed.

Javier walked toward the sedan and van.

Matt turned the handle on the service door to the garage, flipped on the lights inside, and he and Frank went in. The overhead fluorescent lights flickered on and shone down on a fleet of dust-covered luxury cars and exotics. Matt hit the button to open the first garage door.

"What's up with Jorge sending a crew?" Frank asked. "That's a hell of a lot of muscle for a couple bags of shit."

"Those couple bags are worth half a million dollars. I'm guessing he wants to make sure that all gets back to him as it should."

"Still," Frank said. "Seems like some kind of show of force or something."

"Just relax, Frank. Everything is good."

"If you say so," Frank said.

The pair stood at the open garage door and guided the van backward. As soon as the van was inside, Javier and another of his guys, dressed in a red floral shirt, walked into the garage. Unlike Javier, the man was wearing a pistol in his belt line.

Two men stepped from the van and went to the back doors. Matt immediately noticed they were wearing guns as well.

Frank stepped to the carpet-cleaning van and popped the rear doors open. Javier's men quickly transferred the four bags from one van to the other.

"That's all of it?" Javier asked.

"Fifty kilos, as agreed," Matt said. "Plus, there's an extra five in there. Call it a tip."

"I'm sure Jorge will like that," Javier said.

The two men who had been loading the van closed the rear doors and waited.

Javier asked the man in the red shirt to go get the satellite phone. "Jorge wanted me to call him once we made the pickup," Javier said. "Elian is going to grab the sat phone quick. We'll make the call, and we should be good."

The man returned with the phone a second later. The two other guys who were in the sedan had returned with him. Matt caught Frank giving him an uneasy face. Frank had his guns on, but Matt was unarmed. Six men, most if not all of them armed, were basically blocking their exit from the garage. Matt tried to put it out of mind. He and Jorge had a deal. They'd done business before. Jorge had delivered on everything to that point without issue.

Matt and Frank waited while Javier dialed. He held the phone to his ear.

"Hey, we got it," Javier said. "It's all there."

Matt couldn't hear the words being spoken on the other end of the call.

"No, not yet," Javier said.

Something else was said that Matt couldn't make out.

"We're ready, yeah," Javier said. "Okay. As soon as you hang up." He held the phone out toward Matt. "He wants to talk to you."

Without a hint of warning, the men all drew their weapons.

"What the hell is this!" Frank shouted.

Matt held his hands up. "What is going on here?"

Five of the six men held Frank and Matt at gunpoint in the garage. Frank grabbed the grips of his pistols holstered under his arms.

"I wouldn't do that," Javier said. He jerked his head at the man named Elian in the red floral shirt. "Get his guns."

Elian disarmed Frank and tossed the weapons into the van on top of the drugs.

Javier pressed the phone into Matt's chest. "Jorge wants to talk to you."

Matt took the phone and slowly brought it to his ear. "What the hell is this?"

"This is your day of reckoning," a voice said. The voice belonged to Jorge.

"Excuse me," Matt said.

"I don't know what the hell your plan was here, but it's done. You're done," Jorge said.

"What are you talking about?"

"Detective Matt Mullin," Jorge said. "Or is it agent? Are you a fed or a cop or both?"

Somehow Jorge had found out his identity. That he was law enforcement. Or at least, had been at one time.

"That was a long time ago that I answered to anyone. Everyone who has done business with me in the last three or four years knows that ain't me. Shit, I have two dead guys in my garden shed as we speak. I put them down myself. We had a deal. You got your payment. Let's finish this."

"See. That's the thing. I thought I was in business with someone in the drug trade. That's easy. All anyone in that game cares about is money. It's easy to know what they're going to do. But the movers and shakers in the drug world are never smart enough to get out while they're ahead. They keep going and going until they eventually get caught or killed. So, when I have you, who I thought was a drug man, looking to cut ties with everything and everyone and get out, I said to myself, 'Finally, a guy smart enough to get out before it's too late.' But the more I thought about it, it just defied too much logic. So, I started digging a little deeper. And wouldn't you know it, as I'm getting these IDs and paperwork together for you, the word comes back that you're an undercover for the feds. I hear that you used to be a cop. And even better, I hear that you must have gone rogue because you're actually living the life. I hear that you've got blood on your hands."

"Walking the line wasn't paying the bills. I got a taste for the finer things. For the other life. I produced a product, made enough money for my brother and me to live the life of luxury for the rest of our days, and now we're getting out. That's all the explanation you need. Like you said, I've got blood on my hands. There's no turning back for me. No turning back for my brother. None of that affects our deal. I shut my whole operation down. Permanently. There's no one talking."

"Yeah, I heard about that. You killed all your own men yesterday, or at least had someone do it for you. Probably that brother of yours. Heard he was some badass marine at one time."

Matt didn't respond.

"See, the whole dynamic has changed," Jorge said. "Now, it looks like I'm apparently in business with a crooked cop or crooked fed. A pig that thinks he's a drug dealer. That thinks he's untouchable because he can play both sides."

"I'm not playing any sides," Matt said. "What you see is what it is."

"Until you're in front of the police. Then I'm sure your tune will change."

"I don't plan on being in front of any police."

"Sorry. It's one of my personal rules. Never trust a crooked cop. Now, my guys are going to take your drugs and your money and then that's that."

"What the hell do you mean 'and that's that'?"

"And then that's the end for you and your brother," Jorge said. "Into the great unknown. Make it easy or hard, but your fate is sealed."

Matt squeezed the phone in his hand. He stared down the barrel of the gun that Javier held a few feet from him. To Javier's left, two more guns were pointed at him. Matt glanced to his right to see Frank, who had eyes locked on the three men aiming pistols at him.

CHAPTER 32

I sent Ryan and Garcia off to meet with the marine unit and see what was going on with the boat. Steve joined Tillerson and me as we headed over to the patrol building to have another chat with tattooed Mr. Fernandez.

"He's walking out of here when we're done?" I asked.

"If he delivers. He claims he has a lot of information," Tillerson said. He pulled open the entrance door to the patrol building, and Steve and I funneled in after him. Tillerson looked over his shoulder and continued. "And if he does give us the information we're after, and gets back out on the streets, he better damn well hope he doesn't push as much as a couple of aspirins. If he sells another anything, he's done. The deal states we'll request a mandatory minimum sentence on his next drug-related offense."

The mandatory minimum sentences started at five years—with priors, Fernandez could be looking at ten years inside with another charge.

We followed Tillerson down the hall, and I spotted Officer Lucerne posted in the hall near the interview and observation room doors.

"Lucerne," I said as we walked up.

"He's in there with an attorney," Officer Lucerne said. "The guy showed maybe ten minutes ago and asked for some privacy."

"All right," Tillerson said. "They've had it. Let's see what's up." He banged his fist on the closed interview room door.

A moment later, the door opened, and a round man in a gray suit emerged. He stepped into the hallway. "Sonny Michaels," he said.

Steve, Tillerson, and I introduced ourselves.

"This guy doesn't want to talk to me at all," Michaels said. "And he doesn't want to listen to anything I suggest. He basically wants me to check the language on a deal and then kick rocks. Though he didn't say kick rocks."

"Yeah, he's not very affable," I said.

"Is there some kind of deal being presented here?" Michaels asked.

"I have it," Tillerson said. He opened his folder and passed a few sheets of paper from it to the public defender.

"Let's go inside, and I'll look this over as we get started," Michaels said.

"How are we doing this?" I asked.

"You come in with me. Ask whatever questions you have," Tillerson said.

Steve pointed to the neighboring door in the hall. "I'll get the observation room."

"Make sure the recording equipment is set," Tillerson said.

215

"Yeah, I got it," Steve said.

Tillerson and I followed the attorney into the room. Fernandez hadn't moved from his spot at the table where I'd seen him hours earlier.

"Do you have my deal?" Fernandez asked.

"Your attorney is looking it over," Tillerson said.

"You mean this hack public defender is looking it over." Fernandez jerked his head at Michaels. "Probably can't get a real job at a firm. Hey, just make sure they ain't screwing me over and then beat it."

Michaels had a seat next to his client, gave him a look of disdain, then started reading the paperwork.

Fernandez stared at him. Tillerson took a seat across from the two at the metal desk. I opted for leaning against the wall near the observation glass.

"It says that if you're convicted of another drug-related offense, they'll request a mandatory minimum sentence. We should get that out of there. That isn't—"

Fernandez held his hand up to silence the public defender. "Does it say I walk out of here if I give them what they're asking for?"

"You could be looking at ten years, minimum, with another charge."

"It doesn't matter. Does it say what it's supposed to?"

"A name and location of the person distributing desomorphine, which is also known by the street name, Krokodil. That information provided by you negates charges of possession with intent of a controlled substance, and distribution of the same."

"Do I walk if I give them this?" Fernandez asked again.

"Is that all that he was brought in on? There isn't something else?" Michaels asked. His eyes went from Tillerson to me.

"That's it," Tillerson said. "Name and location and he walks out like this latest charge never happened. But again, a repeat offense and the DA's office is going to request a lengthy sentence."

"It doesn't matter. I'm getting the hell out of here. Moving back to Monterrey," Fernandez said. He looked at the public defender. "You can go."

"I'd probably advise against that," Michaels said.

"You served your purpose. I'm through with you," Fernandez said.

"Suit yourself," Michaels said. He pushed the papers toward Tillerson, stood, and walked from the room.

"The last time a public defender helped me out, I ended up serving a year," Fernandez said. "On something that I should have spent maybe a month inside on."

"We're waiting on that name," Tillerson said.

"Manny Jimenez," Fernandez said. "Dominican dude. Bigger. Got shoulder-length dreads. That's your guy."

A Manuel Jimenez was one of the deceased at the old horse-racing practice facility. One of the guys who had taken a round to the back of the head and another pair in the back. Tillerson turned on his chair and looked over his shoulder at me.

"Manuel Jimenez is dead," I said. "We found him at that old horse track yesterday, with Tavaras."

"With Tavaras?" Fernandez asked. "Why the hell would they be together at a horse track?"

I didn't have an answer for him, not that I'd give it to him if I did. "The name of a dead guy isn't doing us much good, Tillerson."

Tillerson turned toward Fernandez. "What are we supposed to do with a dead guy's name?"

"That ain't my problem," Fernandez said. "Where on that deal does it say that the guy needs to be breathing? Show me that."

It didn't, but the name still wasn't giving us anything.

"What else do you know about this Jimenez?" Tillerson asked.

"He was doing everything with the Krokodil. He was Carlos's contact. Lived in some big ass estate over on Key Biscayne."

"Key Biscayne?" Tillerson asked.

"Yeah."

"Where on Key Biscayne?"

"I don't have an address for you if that's what you're looking for. I just heard it was on the water near the park on the south side. There's a little inlet there. I guess it's right on that. At least, that's what Tavaras said. He mentioned it, and I'd commented that I knew where that was. When I was a kid, we used to fish over there."

"Give us a second," Tillerson said. He rose from his chair and waved for me to follow him from the interview room. Tillerson closed the door, and we entered the observation room.

"I pulled up Jimenez's sheet again," Steve said. "He's got a North Miami Beach address, not Key Biscayne."

"Yeah. We've got a problem," Tillerson said.

"What?" I asked.

"I can't say anything without checking something out first. Give me ten minutes. If you want to continue questioning him, go ahead. I have to make a couple phone calls."

"Care to clue us in?" I asked.

"Just…" Tillerson undid the top button on his dress shirt. He tugged at his tie. His face looked redder than it had a few minutes prior. "I'll be back." He walked from the room.

"What the hell was that about?" Steve asked.

"I don't know. Something with the address got him all frazzled," I said.

"You want to wait or go back in?" Steve asked.

"Go back in. I want to see what else he knows."

Steve gave me a nod, and I returned to the interview room next door. I took a seat across from Fernandez. "So, Manuel Jimenez went by Manny?"

"Yeah," Fernandez said.

"How long were these two in business?" I asked. "Tavaras and Manny." I took out my notepad and waited for his response.

"Since the Krokodil started hitting the streets. Just about a year," Fernandez said.

"Do you know how Tavaras and Manny met?" I asked.

"I think they knew each other or something. I don't know."

"Did you get the impression that this Manny was in charge?"

"There's always somebody above somebody," Fernandez said. "But I don't know. He normally had some guys with him who seemed to answer to him. I don't know what their names were. Muscle. Big guys. Both white. Bald."

"Sure," I said. From the description, I imagined the big guys he spoke of were Eric Rossi and Paul Lattore. "And how often did Tavaras meet with this Manny?"

"I don't know. A couple of times," Fernandez said. He lifted his chained hands and scratched at the "hu$tle" tattoo on his forehead. "I couldn't give you an exact number."

"And just to confirm, this Manny was selling Tavaras the Krokodil?" I asked.

He didn't respond.

"They're both dead," I said.

"Yeah, that's what he was doing. Am I free to go?" he asked.

"That I can't tell you. You'll have to wait until the other guy gets back. He's in charge of that part of things."

"I mean, I told you what you guys wanted to know."

"I know you did," I said. "Can I just ask you a few more questions until he gets back? We should be able to get this wrapped up then."

"Yeah, whatever," Fernandez said.

"Did you know of these real estate guys that were trying to get a meeting with whoever ran the Krokodil?" I asked.

"Yeah, someone brought a pair of guys to Tavaras. I'm not sure who. They had a distribution channel that they wanted to pitch to the Krokodil guys. Wait, those two didn't clip Tavaras, did they?"

The fact that he asked, and the way he asked it, made me believe that he didn't know Frost and Nance were law enforcement.

"I don't think so," I said.

The door of the room opened, and Tillerson waved me out. I excused myself from Fernandez and left the room. Tillerson walked into the observation room and, after I stepped inside behind him, closed the door.

"We've got a problem. A bad one," Tillerson said. He sat on the edge of the table where Steve sat.

"Yeah, you said that before you left," I said. "What's the issue?"

"It's either a hell of a coincidence or the property that he's speaking of on Key Biscayne belongs to the feds."

"What?" I asked.

"What the hell does that mean?" Steve asked.

"As in, owned by the bureau."

"I'm still lost," I said.

"Through a handful of shell companies and fronts, an estate on Key Biscayne owned by the FBI is being leased to a Matt Haynes. Matt Haynes is actually Matt Mullin, who used to work for Vice."

"The undercover fed you've been communicating with?" I asked.

"Yeah, or at least trying to communicate with. He's never called me back after the last time I reached out."

"Why would Fernandez think that Manny Jimenez lived there?" I asked.

"I don't know," Tillerson said. "Has to be a reason, though. I just called my contact at the bureau to see if he knew anything. He said he didn't but was going to ask around."

"Did you ask if they were familiar with Jimenez?"

"I did, and the name didn't ring any bells."

"Think this Mullin might be doing something with the feds and Krokodil?"

Tillerson shrugged. "I don't know."

"Well, wait. What makes you think that the house is where Fernandez is talking about?" I asked. "I mean, Key Biscayne is small, but it's not that small."

"The place he described is exactly where the feds have Mullin staying. There's maybe a hundred houses off that little inlet by the park. What do you think the odds would be that Mullin wouldn't have a clue that this was going on in his neighborhood?"

"Probably pretty slim," Steve said. "Doesn't mean it wasn't, though."

"Yeah, but I can't help but think it's all connected somehow," Tillerson said.

"So, what are we doing? Are we trying to go there and have a chat with him, or what do you want to do?" I asked.

"I don't know," Tillerson said. "We risk blowing his cover if we just pop in to talk. We will one hundred percent piss off the feds if we go there unannounced. I'm not sure what's the best route here. But we need to figure it out. We're going to need to talk to him. Questions need to be answered."

CHAPTER 33

"We've got a body here," Garcia said.

I held my cell phone to my ear and got behind the wheel of an unmarked cruiser in the station's lot.

"COD?" I asked as I fired the engine. Steve hopped in the cruiser's passenger side.

"Three shots, center mass," Garcia said. "No signs of forced entry. We looked in the front glass of the marina office and could see the guy's feet sticking out from a back hall. We got inside and confirmed the man deceased. He's lying in a little back room that has a bed and television in it. There's a refrigerator and hot plate next to the sink. Guessing this guy was living here."

"Did anyone see anything?" I asked.

"Not that we found yet. By the looks of the body, I'm guessing this happened last night sometime. There's a couple people lingering around outside that Ryan went to talk to. They seem to be locals. Maybe we can get a positive ID from one of them, get a location of a nearby camera, at least give us something to work with. I can't imagine it's a coincidence that there's a DB where we find the boat we figure to be involved with Frost and Nance. This is probably related to the rest of this garbage."

I put the cruiser in reverse and pulled from the parking spot. I drove forward to the lot's exit and caught Tillerson in a cruiser in my rearview mirror. "I would imagine it is. What's up with the boat itself?"

"It looks like it's the one we were looking for. No tags on it. The marine unit is going to drag it back to our marina so Colt and the guys can have a look at it."

"Okay," I said.

"What do you guys have going on?" Garcia asked.

"Not sure yet," I said. "We got a little information from the guy that we had over at the patrol building. He said Manuel Jimenez was behind the Krokodil."

"We have that guy, right? Dead at the old horse track?"

I pulled out into traffic and headed for the tollway. "Yeah, but where he said the guy lived is an issue. Apparently, we have a federal UC residing where this Fernandez thought Jimenez lived."

"How does that work?"

"I don't know. But we're going to find out. Tillerson and another one of his guys, Parnell, are following us out to the property. We're going to try to pick him up. Tillerson got the okay from the bureau to bring him in, and we got some bogus paperwork drawn up saying that he's wanted for questioning for something that ties into his cover. It's basically just a paper trail if anyone ever questioned why the police were at the house."

"The feds are allowing us to bring in one of theirs?"

"They'll be there when we talk to him," I said.

"Is he supposed to be there alone?" Garcia asked.

"We don't know. Could be a couple more people." I merged right and entered the tollway, headed south. The drive to Key Biscayne would take us the better part of forty-five minutes. "Tillerson asked the feds who was normally at the house. They said it wasn't something that they monitored."

"So, there could be a dozen armed people there?" Garcia asked.

"I sure as hell hope not. This is an affluent area. I'm guessing the neighbors wouldn't take well to armed men in their fancy neighborhood. I'm hoping this Mullin answers the door, is put off that we're there, and comes along to answer our questions without any bullshit."

"Well, if you need us, give us a buzz. I need to get on the horn with Colt and get someone out here to go over this place. I'm sure he's going to be thrilled that we have another scene for him."

"And the boat to go over," I said.

"Yeah, that too."

"All right. Keep me updated," I said.

"Will do."

I ended the call and dropped my phone into my lap.

"Another body?" Steve asked.

"Yeah."

"And obviously connected to the rest of this mess," Steve said.

"More than likely. They're thinking it's our boat."

"Did anyone see anything?"

"Garcia said that there were a couple—" My cell phone rang in my lap. The screen showed the station was calling. "Damn. This is probably Halloway."

"Are you going to answer it?"

I thought about it for another ring or two—I hadn't told him what we were doing.

"Damn," I said. "Yeah." I lifted my phone and swiped Talk. "Harrington."

"Where are you, and what are you guys doing?" the captain asked.

"Picking up a federal UC that we think may be involved in this somehow."

"A federal UC?" he asked.

"Correct. They gave us the okay."

"Walsh?" he asked.

"Steve is with me. Ryan and Garcia are over at a marina in North Miami, not too far from where Frost and Nance's bodies were found."

"I hear they've got a body there," Halloway said.

"A body and what we think is the boat we were looking for. The scene there seems connected to all of this."

"And this guy you're going to talk to?" the captain asked. "What do you think the odds of a development with him are?"

"I'd say pretty good if he talks."

"How do we think he's connected?" Halloway asked.

I gave the captain the details from our talk with Mr. Fernandez. He agreed that it would have been a hell of a coincidence that everything was happening around Mullin, and in his own neighborhood, without him having a clue what was going on.

"I'm going to make a phone call," Halloway said. "Try to push the DEA off for another day. Say we've had a couple developments and need some more time to put everything together for them."

"Think that's going to work?" I asked.

"We'll see," he said. "Either way, if they come looking and you guys are all out working, what are they going to do? Stand here and wait? Doesn't sound like a good use of government dollars to me. Get to work," the captain said. "Get us something today."

"Thanks, Cap," I said. "I'll give you a ring with an update when I have one."

"Yup," he said and hung up.

I continued the drive, with Tillerson never leaving my rearview mirror for more than a minute or two at a time. A few small pockets of traffic on I-95 south extended our forty-minute drive another ten. We drove the Rickenbacker Causeway onto Virginia Key and then crossed the Bear Cut Bridge onto Key Biscayne. The navigation running in the car told me that the address was on the far end of the island. I followed its prompts to get there, never running into any guard shack or gate, which I thought odd for a high-dollar neighborhood in Florida.

We rolled up to the property, one of two at the end of the street, right at one o'clock. All I could see was a closed black iron gate over a redbrick driveway. Thick landscaping blocked any view of a house. I pulled past the gates and threw the cruiser into Park at the edge of the street. Steve and I stepped out as Tillerson pulled up behind our car.

"This is the place, eh?" I asked.

Tillerson swung his door closed. "This is it."

Parnell, mid-forties with a jet-black widow's peak, stepped from Tillerson's cruiser. He looked around and whistled. "Heck of a neighborhood," he said. Parnell swung his passenger door closed and stretched his back. He wore a short-sleeved button-up shirt, slacks, and a badge on his hip.

"Call button?" Steve asked.

"I imagine there's one at the gate," I said.

Our group headed over. Inside the double gates, the driveway took an immediate right. The orientation of the driveway, combined with the thick landscaping, blocked any view inside the property, and I imagined the layout was by design. To the left and right of the gates was a six- or seven-foot-high concrete wall creating a perimeter around the grounds. My eyes went to the call box at car-window level off to the left of the driveway. I hit the button on the box, and we waited. No one answered. I spotted the red light of a camera at the top pillar of the gates and wondered if someone inside was watching us and choosing not to answer.

"You can see where the driveway goes from over here," Steve said.

He stood near the metal gates. He had his shoulder pressed against the concrete wall. Steve took another step into the bushes. "I got a silver sedan near what looks like a fountain. I have another vehicle behind it. All I can see is the nose. Looks like a black van."

"People?" Tillerson asked.

"Not seeing any," Steve said. "The front of the house looks open." Steve stepped from the bushes. "Looks like a little under a hundred yards away."

I hit the call button again.

"Anyone want to get a look?" Steve asked.

"Yeah, let me see what you were looking at," Tillerson said. He headed over to where Steve had been and tucked himself into the bushes for a view. "I see the vehicles," he said. "Yeah, looks like that door is open. Hit the call again."

"I just did," I said.

"Lay on the damn thing. It looks like someone is here," Tillerson said.

I pressed the button a few more times, but still no one answered. I walked toward the gates, to where Steve and Tillerson had been, to try to look into the property for myself. Tillerson gave me the area. I craned my neck left and right, but aside from the vehicles and a small section of the house with an open door, I didn't see much else.

"What's the move here?" Parnell asked.

I left the gate area and went back to the group gathered in the driveway outside the gate.

Tillerson walked fast to the call box and jammed the button down repeatedly. "I ain't leaving until we get some damn answers," he said.

CHAPTER 34

Matt

With Javier's gun trained on him, Matt carried a bag from the boat, around the side of the house, and to the back of his carpet-cleaning van parked just outside the garage. Javier took it upon himself to commandeer the van to be used as additional transport after they'd filled their own van with drugs and money. Matt stacked the bag on top of another bag inside the back of the van. He looked toward the cab. The keys were hanging from the van's ignition.

"A couple more runs," Javier said. "Thanks for having another van here for us. Looks like you boys had more money than we thought."

Matt said nothing and turned to walk toward the water again. He saw Frank approaching, also at gunpoint, carrying another duffel bag stuffed with money. Javier had been using Frank and Matt for the heavy lifting before inevitably putting a bullet in their heads, or at least that was what Matt figured he would do.

The money-filled bags and boxes were quickly dwindling

inside the boat. In another few trips, all the cash would be loaded. Matt had been going over his options for escape while he made the last trips back and forth across the property. Time was ticking away, and a decision on what to do would have to come fast. Two of the men Jorge sent were already inside the house, pilfering valuables. The other two seemed to be trying to get one of the Lamborghinis to start. Matt imagined they had designs of taking it.

Matt went around the pool where he'd spent hours and hours each day. The days of sitting around talking to women and getting drunk were gone. He passed the pool shed where several men had lost their lives. Matt wondered when the two guys inside would be found. Javier followed him toward the water. Matt stepped onto the dock and walked to the left toward the yacht. He glanced down at the water, across the channel, then at the park. He contemplated diving in and swimming for a neighboring house or the park across the water, yet he envisioned getting shot in the back of the head the second he came up for air.

"Get your ass on the boat," Javier said.

Matt used the dock's ladder, took two steps down, then stepped onto the stern of the fifteen-year-old Ocean Yachts Odyssey. The yacht, sixty-five foot and probably still worth a half million dollars, came with the house, the cars, and everything else the bureau provided. As with the cars, Matt normally didn't want the vessel seen, and until the prior day, it had been stored at Roger's marina. Matt had always thought there was a possibility of the yacht or vehicles coming back as being owned by the FBI. He didn't like the fact that they'd all been repossessed locally. It left the chance that someone could recognize one of them and blow his cover or, at the very minimum, ask some questions. He also had a sneaking suspicion that the vehicles and yacht could be tracked.

Matt thought about the gun in his suitcase. He stepped up into the salon and through the galley. Matt glanced over his shoulder several times to see the barrel of Javier's pistol, never more than an arm's reach from the back of his head. He'd never be able to get to his gun before being shot—he'd need to disarm Javier first. Matt had considered a quick swipe backward at the weapon, hoping the element of surprise might work to his benefit. Yet every time he thought of doing that, he imagined getting shot in the face. And even if he did manage to disarm Javier, he would need to eliminate him as a threat before the guy holding Frank at gunpoint neared the yacht and saw what was going on.

Matt let out a hard breath as he stepped down the stairs and entered one of the spare staterooms. The room, which hours earlier had been filled with almost fifty million in cash, had only a few boxes and bags remaining. Matt scooped up a box that said "1" on the side and turned around.

"Looks like a good box there," Javier said. "Maybe I just have you put that one into my car."

Javier must have put two and two together and figured out the numbers on the sides of the boxes and bags indicated the value of the drugs within. A one signified a million, and the ones marked with .25 and .5 signified a quarter million or half. Matt didn't respond to Javier's comment.

Javier stepped to the side and let him pass. Matt carried the box of mostly hundreds off the yacht and set it up on the dock. He climbed the ladder, scooped the box in his arms, and started up the dock. Matt looked toward the shore and saw Frank appear, with Elian in his red floral shirt following a foot or two behind. The groups passed, and with as much precision as he could, Matt mouthed the words "Take the van" to his brother. His eyes quickly went to Elian to see if he'd seen the signal. He hadn't, yet Matt didn't know if his point had been made to Frank. Either way, getting inside that van was their only chance of escape.

"Shit," Matt said. He dropped his box to the ground, spilling the bound stacks of hundreds across the grass.

"Pick that shit up," Javier said. He shoved Matt down and kept his aim on him.

Matt shook his head and gathered the money. He glanced toward the dock and the water as he stacked the cash back into the box—he was trying to buy time. Trying to give Frank time to catch up. But Frank wasn't coming.

"Let's go. I ain't got all day," Javier said.

Matt stuffed the last few stacks of cash into the box and replaced the cardboard lid. He lifted the box from the ground and, with a shove from Javier, started toward the front of the house. He again glanced over his shoulder. Frank still wasn't coming. Matt rounded the corner of the house and walked to the van out front. The noise of a car's thundering exhaust came a split second later—the guys must have gotten one of the cars running.

As Matt passed the open garage door, he looked in to see

that the two men had moved deeper into the garage to try their luck on another car. He glanced toward the house but didn't see either of the other two men who had gone inside. Matt went to the van's back doors and set the box down. He quickly glanced toward the side of the house. Frank was crouched at the home's corner. There was no Elian. Frank quickly waved at him to continue.

Matt took a step back from the van and fired an elbow backward at eye level. The blow hit home and sent Javier stumbling—nothing had ever felt more satisfying. Matt turned and kicked Javier's hand with everything he had. The gun flew from his grip. Thumping footsteps across the ground drew Matt's attention. In a full run, Frank dove at Javier and tackled him to the ground. With five or six downward strikes with his forearm, Frank put Javier out cold and spit in his face. Matt's eyes shot to the garage. He couldn't see the men inside, but they weren't coming out.

Frank scooped up Javier's gun and closed the van's rear doors. Matt went for the driver's seat and jumped inside. He fired the engine as Frank jumped into the passenger side.

"Where's the Elian guy?" Matt asked.

"Dead. Now let's get the hell out of here," Frank said.

Matt yanked the van into Drive and planted the gas pedal to the floor. The tires spun, and the van shot forward. Matt looked left at the house to see the two men emerge from inside. They were shouting and drawing weapons.

"Get down!" Frank shouted. He reached over and pulled Matt lower.

Matt followed the turn in the driveway, trying to stay as

low as he could. He kept the gas down and pointed the fishtailing van in the direction of the front gates. Matt's ears were filled by gunshots followed by the rounds plinking through the van's metal.

CHAPTER 35

"What the hell is that?" Tillerson asked.

I didn't imagine he was looking for an answer. We all heard what he was talking about—squealing tires and a racing engine.

"Shit! Get away from the gates!" Steve shouted. He jumped from the bushes and retreated to the street as he pulled his service weapon.

Tillerson, Parnell, and I followed suit.

By the time I got my weapon's sights up on the gate, I heard gunfire and then what sounded like crunching metal. The sound of the racing engine remained, yet no vehicle approached the gate. More gunfire came, and the engine noise went silent. Above the tops of trees and bushes making up the landscaping, I saw a plume of smoke and dust.

"In," I said.

We ran to the gates, and I pushed one while Steve pulled the other. The point where the two met spread far enough for Tillerson and Parnell to squeeze through. The pair spread them from the other side, allowing Steve and me to pass, Steve's squeeze a little tighter than my own. We started around the corner of the driveway, guns up and at the ready. More gunfire caught my ear. We got low and held our position, just twenty feet inside the gate.

Rounds from the continuing gunfire tinked and slapped off their intended target, a rolled-on-its-side, full-size cargo van lying in the grass beside the driveway. My eyes were fixed on the area a hundred feet away. The van's nose faced us, and the undercarriage was toward what I could see of the house. From our spot, we couldn't see the shooter or shooters—the view being basically the same, or worse, than it was from the gate. Color caught my eye at the van's nose. An armed man was taking cover behind the hood. He noticed us and disappeared. Another man, unarmed, came into view a split second later.

The guy held his hands up. "FBI," he said.

I couldn't tell if it was a statement or a question.

"That's Mullin," Tillerson said. "Mullin!" he shouted. "It's Tillerson!" He took a step forward.

Mullin held his hand out, telling him to hold his spot. Tillerson stopped.

"Give me the situation!" Tillerson called. He turned toward Parnell. "Call this in."

Parnell pulled his phone from his pocket.

"Five men, armed," Mullin said. "They're taking cover behind a pair of vehicles next to the garages."

More gunfire came, this time aimed in our direction. Bullets ripped through the Bird of Paradise trees and palms planted at the driveway's edge. Leaves, bark, and dirt flew just ten feet ahead of where we were hunkered down. The guys were shooting blind at where they figured we were. We needed some real cover and a position where we could return fire.

"What are they armed with?" Parnell asked.

"Handguns," Mullin said. "No rifles. We've got a line of sight on them but only have one weapon. Just a couple rounds left."

"Hang tight!" Tillerson called out. He turned toward our group. "I'm going to go to that van, give them a little help, and get some eyes on just what the hell we're dealing with here. Someone give me some cover."

Parnell said he had him, and the pair stepped forward. Parnell brought his weapon up, took another couple quick steps, and put rounds on the spot the men were firing from. Tillerson broke into a run for the van the moment Parnell began laying down cover fire. Tillerson shot a few times as he ran and then ducked in behind the van's hood. Parnell retreated to Steve and me.

"What are we looking at?" I asked.

"I only saw two guys at the silver sedan. I put fire on both but I think I put the leading guy down," Parnell said.

Gunfire ripped through the bushes five feet from us. We went belly down. I heard the whiz of a round come right over my head. Shredded bits of tree bark landed on the back of my suit jacket. The gunfire stopped. Shooting blind or not, they had our position.

"We have to get to cover," Steve said.

The van was our closest option. We were about to make a run for it when automatic gunfire shredded the tree line behind us. It had to have been thirty shots.

"That isn't a damn handgun," I said. I stayed on my belly and army crawled forward fifteen feet to try to get a look at our shooters. I reached the edge of the landscaping. A pygmy palm surrounded by twenty or more basketball-sized rocks stood to my left. Tropical grass surrounded the base of the tree, providing some camouflage. I crawled into the grass and got a look at our shooters from behind the cover of the rocks. A man in a floral shirt had an assault rifle over the roof of the sedan and aimed it at the van. I brought up my sights, let out a breath, got my aim, and fired off three rounds. He reached for his neck and dropped from view. A split second later, another man emerged with his rifle aimed in my direction. I went flat, and the gunfire started. Dirt flew all around me. The gun's rounds cracked off the rocks where I was taking cover. Shots came from my right, from the van. The incoming gunfire on me stopped. I didn't try to get a look. I crawled backward to Parnell and Steve and crouched next to the two.

"Did Tillerson put the shooter down?" Steve asked.

I shook my head. "I don't know, but I think I got the first one," I said. "We still need to get to that van."

"Let's go," Steve said. "Get Tillerson to cover us."

We got in position to make the run for the van and whistled over. Neither Tillerson, Mullin, nor the other guy was in view. A second later, Tillerson emerged from the back side of the van and put rounds on the car while the two other guys made a break for the back of the house. The moment Mullin and the other guy were clear, Tillerson took cover again behind the van. Return fire came at him. One of the van's tires popped and hissed air. Another round went ricocheting off something beneath the van and cracked off the concrete wall to our right.

"What was that?" Steve asked. "Where the hell did those two just run off to?"

"Tillerson," I called.

He appeared, crouched at the hood of the van.

"We're coming over," I said. "Give us a little cover fire."

"You got it," he said.

We made a break for it as soon as Tillerson began firing and met him at the van. Tillerson dropped the magazine from his weapon. "I'm out," he said. "That was my second magazine."

"Standard issue?" I asked.

"Yeah," Tillerson said.

I pulled my extra magazine from my shoulder holster and passed it to him. "Make them count."

"Appreciate it," Tillerson said.

"Where did those two go?" I asked. "What the hell did we roll up on?"

"I don't know. Mullin just said that these guys were from some cartel."

"Where did they go?" I asked.

"Mullin and the other guy grabbed some bags from the back of the van and said to cover them. They made a break for the rear of the property. They were already in full run before I could even respond."

"How many are left?" I asked. "How many shooters?"

"Just two. And I saw one of the two run for the backyard,"

Tillerson said. "I think the guy who is still over there is shot."

Three gunshots rang out in succession. Someone shouted. Another pair of gunshots came from behind the house.

Parnell rolled around the nose of the van, had a look, fired two shots, and came back to us. "Four down between the van over there and the car. Let's go see what the hell is going on in the back."

We left the cover of the van, weapons up, and walked to the silver sedan and black cargo van. As we neared, I saw both vehicles were riddled with bullet holes. We went man-to-man on the ground and disarmed and cuffed each. It was procedure but useless since all the men were dead.

"Someone has to keep eyes on the front of this place," I said.

"We got it," Tillerson said.

"We should have backup here any second," Parnell added.

"All right. Come on," I said and waved for Steve to follow. We continued to the side of the home, kept our backs to the house, and followed the southern wall until it opened into a big backyard facing the water. To the left ahead of us, a hundred feet away, was a white outbuilding about the size of a two-car garage. To our right was a big pool area and outdoor kitchen and bar. Straight ahead was the edge of the property and what looked like a dock that wrapped around it. Farther right appeared a man-made beach of white sand. We continued around the pool and took a path in the grass toward the water. I spotted a man in a blue floral shirt facedown in the grass where the grass met the dock. A pistol lay just a foot from his hand. I kicked it away as we passed.

I didn't need to check for a pulse. He had an exit wound the size of a baseball on the left side of his head.

Directly to our right was the beach I'd spotted. To the left, the dock stemming off the seawall continued to wrap around the grounds. The top of a big fishing boat or yacht was visible through some of the bushes. I stepped onto the dock and followed it around the corner. A big white yacht was tied at the end of the dock with its stern facing us. The engines fired, and I caught movement up on the flybridge. The other man who'd been with Mullin emerged from the cabin of the yacht. He looked at us and began feverishly untying the ship.

"Hey," I shouted. I glanced at Steve, who was on my heels. "These two are trying to get out of here."

I jogged down the dock, my gun up and my sights on the guy who continued to untie the yacht. He tossed one mooring line and quickly moved to another.

"Hey, let me see them hands!" I called. I stopped twenty feet from him and repeated my command.

The guy didn't stop what he was doing.

Mullin appeared from the upper deck. "We're in the middle of an operation with the FBI. We can't be caught here. It'll blow our cover," he said.

The sound of feet thumping the dock behind me caught my attention.

"What the hell is going on, Mullin?" Tillerson asked.

"You have to let us get out of here, Tillerson. I'll fill you in on everything as soon as the bureau will let me."

"That isn't how this is going to go," Tillerson said. "We

need you to come in and answer some questions. The feds will be there. They gave us the okay to bring you in on this."

"On what?" Mullin asked.

I kept eyes on the guy with Mullin who was untying the ropes. He looked cagey, like he was about to do something.

"Why don't you two hop off the boat," I said. "It's just us here."

"Sorry," Mullin said. "We have to go. You guys should too. These guys will have friends coming."

The guy threw the last line off the boat. "We're free," he shouted up toward Mullin.

"Mullin. Get off that boat!" Tillerson shouted.

"You're going to get us killed, Tillerson," Mullin shouted. "Get the hell out of here."

The boat began to drift, an inch or two at a time, from the dock. My mind raced. If Mullin and the other guy sailed off into the sunset, we'd be sitting on yet another scene with a pile of dead bodies and not a single answer. The case would get tossed to the DEA, and we'd be left with nothing but unanswered questions.

My decision was made. I took a few quick steps to the end of the dock, jumped the three-foot gap that had grown between the dock and the yacht, and landed on the swim platform. The second my feet landed, the yacht's engines came alive. Someone, which could only have been Mullin, had opened the throttle. I grabbed the railing to keep my balance, scooped up one of the mooring lines the guy had untied, and tossed the line toward the dock at Steve and Tillerson. The rope landed a few feet from Steve. As he went for it, I watched it get pulled into the water. I turned and aimed my weapon at where the guy who'd untied the yacht had sat down. He was gone.

Mullin, at the helm, had made a turn and pointed the bow toward the bay. We passed the dock I'd leapt from. Steve and Tillerson stood at the end, twenty yards away, staring at me. Steve held up his hands as if questioning what the hell to do next.

"Get the marine unit," I shouted. The twenty yards turned into forty. Then sixty.

He shouted something back through cupped hands, but I couldn't make it out. The pair quickly grew smaller and smaller as we made our way toward the bay's waters. I focused my attention up at the flybridge.

"Mullin!" I shouted.

He appeared on the flybridge deck and looked down at me.

"Lieutenant Harrington. Miami Homicide. Kill it!" I ordered.

"I know who you are, and I can't, Lieutenant," he said. "Come inside. I'll meet you in the salon."

"What the hell is a salon?" I asked.

"Just come inside." He disappeared from his spot on the deck above me.

I walked up the steps from the swim platform, crossed the lower deck, and entered the cabin of the yacht. The moment I put a foot inside, I caught a flash of color from the corner of my eye.

CHAPTER 36

"What are we going to do with him?" I heard.

"We don't have a ton of options now, do we, Frank? What the hell were you thinking?"

I squinted hard, trying to get my vision. I caught a glimpse of someone seated in front of me.

"I was thinking that a damn cop jumped on our boat and we needed to take care of it, Matt," I heard.

I shook my head, squinted again, and got some focus. The left side of my face and neck were warm and wet from blood. Mullin was seated on a chair in front of me.

"Wake up," I heard. The voice came from Mullin's guy, presumably named Frank, who was seated to my right. He smacked me in the side of the face with the back of his hand.

I got a look at my surroundings. I was on a small sofa in the yacht's main cabin. The kitchen was off to my right, and the water was off the stern of the yacht to my left. I didn't know how long I'd been out, but I still saw slivers of land. We were stopped—anchored.

Someone had to have set me on the sofa. I looked down, and there was blood on the left side of my suit, but I wasn't restrained with anything. My hands and legs were free. I noticed my weapon wasn't in my holster. I put my hand down on the couch cushion to push myself up, but a hand from the Frank guy next to me planted me back into the seat. Mullin, in front of me, held my service weapon in his hand. It was pointed at me.

"You're good right there," Mullin said. He leaned forward and snapped his fingers in front of my face. "Are you with it?"

I'd gotten enough of my bearings back to look him dead in the eye. "Yeah, and you better hand me my gun," I said. "Nice and slow."

Mullin shook his head. "Nah," he said. "See, I was going to feed you some more 'We're working with the FBI' bullshit and dump your ass off on the nearest dock, but my genius brother, Frank, decided to pistol-whip you instead."

"How many times do I have to say it?" his brother, apparently, said. "I'm sorry already. I just reacted."

"Go and get some rope or something," Mullin said.

Frank rose from his spot beside me. "Don't bark orders at me."

"Just get something to tie him up with," Mullin said.

"Whatever," his brother replied as he walked out of the cabin.

"Yeah, as I was saying," Mullin said. "My dumbass brother clocking you on the head kind of blew the whole acting-friendly thing out of the water. So now you're getting tied up and dumped over the edge of the boat."

"What the hell are you doing?" I asked. "You're a cop, Mullin."

"Matt Mullin the cop is long gone. He checked out a long time ago. After him, I was Matt Haynes for a couple years. He wasn't much more than a pawn for the FBI. Nah, life started when I decided to be my own man and make my own money."

I dismissed his statement about who he was and wasn't. "Did you kill Frost and Nance?" I asked. "I assume somehow you're wrapped up in all of this bullshit."

"Yeah, I killed them," Mullin said. He didn't elaborate.

"That's it?" I asked. "You killed them? An officer killing two of his own and that's all you have to say?"

"What do you want me to tell you?"

"Why? Why are you doing any of this?"

"Money. Because I'm the criminal that Vice and the FBI wanted," Mullin said. "That they created. Tell me. How many years have to pass before being undercover turns into just living your life? Before you stop pretending and start being?"

I didn't respond.

"Do you think I could ever go back to a regular-Joe life after living in this world they created for me? I eat steak and lobster every day, and I'm not talking about the shit fillets you can get from the grocery store—I'm talking wagyu beef. I drink my fill of top-shelf liquor every night. I have women on call—blondes, brunettes, redheads, whatever. Mansions and servants. The bureau gave me a free pass to all of that. A year or so ago, I started thinking about what would happen when I'm no longer of use to them. I'm supposed to go back to a fifty-five- thousand-dollar-a-year job trying to juggle a mortgage and car payment? Try to find a date online while I'm working sixty hours a week? I don't think so. They wanted a criminal, so I became one. I built an empire in a little over a year. Made a hundred million dollars. In a damn year. I did that."

I shook my head. "Whatever the hell you're talking about, I don't care. What I want to know is why the hell would you take two officers' lives? You were a cop, a fed. There has to be something there. Something that would make you not kill two of your own."

"Two of my own? You keep saying that. You're kidding, right? Those two would have put me away the first chance they got. Do you think that they didn't recognize me the second they showed up at my house? We worked in the same unit for Vice. I couldn't kill those two idiots quick enough. If you're looking for someone to blame, blame Tillerson. He's really the one who killed them. He's the one who put me onto the guys. Told me they were investigating the Krokodil in the area. Said the two were trying to pose as real estate developers with a distribution channel. He asked me to vouch for them. I mean, come on. That's the best that Vice could come up with?" Mullin shook his head.

I had nothing to say to him. All I could focus on was how to get my gun without getting shot.

"You want to hear how it went down?"

"I don't care. You killed them. You'll pay."

Mullin rolled his eyes at me. "Yeah, yeah, I'll pay all right. I bet you want to know. I know I would. So, check this out. I had my guys bring these two idiots to me at the house. And like I said, they recognized me right away. I got them away from my guys under the pretense that I wanted to have a talk with them. So I get the guys to join me out in the shed. We get inside and I tell them I'm working undercover for the feds. Said my guys knew they were cops, but I was going to get them out of there. I told them I just needed to know what they had and where it was so we could retrieve it. The guys gave me everything. Said they had a file but nothing as far as solid leads. Told me how long they'd been working the case, where they were staying. Told me that Vice was trying to find out more about the Krokodil we'd been cooking. After they spilled it, I killed them both. Frost and then Nance. Real quick, one after the other. They never even reacted when I pulled my gun. Like they couldn't believe I would do it. At least I dropped them off for you so you guys knew they were dead and their families could get their benefits."

His words were cold. I didn't hear an ounce of remorse. There was no one around that Mullin needed to keep a cover for. He held my gun, aimed at me. I had no reason to believe he wasn't going to do exactly what he said he would, tie me up and dump me in the water. Whether he planned to shoot me to go along with tossing me off the yacht didn't matter. I wouldn't last long, if at all, in the water if I was restrained— I wasn't the strongest swimmer to begin with.

My mind raced. I looked at my gun—it needed to be in my hand if I was going to have a chance of surviving. I knew either he or his brother had to have another gun as well. The guy with the hole in his head down by the dock at the house didn't get that way by himself. My eyes rose to Mullin's, which were fixed on me. He and his brother were separated, and that was my window. I imagined I'd be tied up the moment the brother returned. I needed to take out Mullin and get my gun.

"All we have is the mooring line," Frank said as he entered the cabin. "I cut, like, six feet off."

My advantage from them being separated had vanished.

"That's fine," Mullin said. "Tie his ass up. Make sure he doesn't get out."

Frank walked around the back of his brother on the chair and again took a seat beside me. "Don't try any bullshit."

With a piece of the rope in each hand, he looped it over me. I needed to do something. Whether I tried to take both brothers out or not, I had to act, or I was done. Frank pulled the two lines he looped over me tight and went to wrap the rope around me again. With everything I had and as quickly as I could, I kicked Mullin's chin. I heard my gun drop and watched him go over in the chair. Immediately, I fired a backward elbow into Frank's face. His hands went for his nose, and I dove to the floor for my weapon. Mullin scrambled to get up.

My eyes landed on my gun just a foot or two from my feet. I took it in hand just as Mullin tackled me to the couch beside Frank. Mullin's arms came around my body, and his hands clasped over mine. He clawed and ripped, trying to take my weapon. His fingernails tore the skin on my hands as he tried to pull my weapon from my grip. Beside us, Frank still pawed at his nose, which was spewing blood down his shirt. He took his hands from his face. A second later, I winced at the blow Frank threw into the side of my head.

"Son of a bitch!" Frank shouted. "You broke my damn nose!" He fired another right into the side of my head, which he'd already opened up when he pistol-whipped me earlier. I couldn't lift my hands to block the strikes without giving up my weapon to Mullin.

"You're dead!" Frank shouted. He threw another fist.

"Kill this prick," Mullin said.

"My pleasure," Frank said.

I saw Frank's hands come toward me and felt him trying to get a grip around my throat. I worked my finger into the trigger guard of my weapon, used all my power to turn the barrel toward Frank, and squeezed off a pair of shots. Frank released his grip on my neck and slid off the couch to the floor. Mullin took a hand from the weapon and started punching me. His one hand on my pistol wasn't going to outpower my two. I got a view of Mullin's brother—he had both hands firmly planted against the two bullet wounds in his side. Blood poured from between his fingers.

Mullin screamed as he flailed rights into the back of my head. I ripped my gun and hands away from his grasp as I turned toward him. Mullin swung again, and I fired a single shot. He stopped midswing and looked down. He put his hand to his side then inspected it as he pulled it away wet with blood. His eyes went to his brother, who'd gone facedown on the floor beside him. Mullin looked at me. He wasn't going to stop his attack. His face said he was prepared to die. It was an outcome that I wasn't prepared to give him.

With Mullin dead, we'd get no answers, and I wanted him to pay for Frost and Nance.

Mullin leaned toward me with a cocked fist. I reached up, took him by the back of the head with my left hand, and drove a right elbow into his face. I felt him go limp. I let Mullin slide to the floor next to his brother and rose from the couch. The half-tied rope that had been around me fell to the floor. I kept the barrel of my weapon on Frank as I checked him for a pulse. I felt something, but it was weak. Blood leaked from him and pooled on the floor beside him. At the rate the blood pool was growing, I didn't imagine he'd be recovering from his wounds.

CHAPTER 37

I checked Mullin and his brother for weapons and took a pistol, presumably the one that I'd been hit with, off Frank. I tucked it into my rear waistline. Mullin remained unconscious. I used the rope that Frank had attempted to tie me up with to tie Mullin's hands and then went to clear the boat. All I found was two duffel bags stuffed with money and another body.

Who the dead man was, I didn't know. The guy was facedown in one of the staterooms. It looked like he'd been beaten and choked to death from the cuts on his face and bruising around his neck. There were no more people on board, which was all I cared about. I returned to the main cabin. Mullin hadn't moved. He was still slumped over his brother's body near the couch. With a bullet wound in Mullin's gut spilling blood, I didn't imagine he was going to give me much fuss when he did regain consciousness. My eyes went to the spiral staircase. I needed to get up to the flybridge to get to the yacht's electronics and make the Mayday call over the radio to the Coast Guard.

I gave Mullin another quick pat down, checked the knot

on the rope around his wrists, and climbed the stairs to the yacht's controls.

My eyes spanned left and right across the cockpit. Three big windows were dead ahead over the dash-like control panel. Six monitors were embedded into the wood dash over a chrome steering wheel and big throttle control. The leftmost screen was a big GPS monitor. I spotted the handheld for the radio clipped on the dash next to the center-mounted captain's chair. I turned and got a look at the rest of the flybridge. A pair of L-shaped couches were on the left and right sides—each had a small table in front of them. A doorway led to some outdoor seating on the upper deck, and a hatch with the ladder went down to the lower one.

I went to the radio, took it in hand, and stretched the coiled cord to the GPS unit. It clearly showed our longitude and latitude. I thumbed down the call button and called a Mayday over the radio. With the Coast Guard on the line, I gave them my location, which turned out to be about five miles east of North Key Largo. They asked my situation, and I did my best to explain. The man on the radio said that they'd been called by the Miami PD marine unit and already had boats out searching for us. After I gave them our location, they said they'd have guys to me in fifteen minutes. I hung the radio on its clip, turned, and walked to the stairs to go back down. A couple of feet from the staircase, I stopped dead.

"Shit," I said under my breath and took a step back. Frank's body was there, but Mullin was no longer slumped over his brother's back. The only thing that remained where Mullin was supposed to be was a loop of bloody rope—the rope that I'd secured his wrists with. The rope wasn't cut, so the blood all over his hands must have allowed him to slip it.

My line of sight—and the sights on my gun—were locked on the staircase. On the flybridge, I was in the worst position I could be in. There was no way I could get down that staircase without presenting the biggest target possible. I craned my neck for a better view of where Mullin had been. A blood trail headed toward the galley and farther into the yacht.

I moved to the left, got a look out the windows, then did the same on the right-hand side of the flybridge—there was nothing to see but water, and no one in it. I stuck to the flybridge's right side, away from the staircase, and headed toward the doorway at the back. I stepped out and put eyes on the hatch with the ladder that led to the lower deck—it didn't give me any better way down than the staircase.

Walking out, I kept my sights on the ladder on the chance that Mullin was there, lying in wait. I saw nothing but the teak deck below. At the short railing of the deck, I got a quick look down—no one was below, no one on the swim platform. My eyes went to the cushions on the couch, six feet below me. My decision was made before even giving it any thought. I swung one leg over the railing, then the other, and stood on the tiny lip of a ledge. I looked down, got my position, and made the jump. The second my feet hit, I felt the pistol that I'd tucked into my rear waistline come free. I quickly tried to grab it, but it fell over the back of the small couch, landed on the swim platform, and slid into the water.

There was nothing I could do. If it was evidence in anything, it was on the bottom of the ocean. I stepped from the couch and aimed my own weapon into the yacht. I got an immediate view of Frank's body yet saw no one else. I stayed low and went toward the door. Remembering getting cracked on the head the last time I'd walked in, I entered low and swung my gun's sights to one corner and then the next. No one was there.

I worked my way through the cabin and into the boat's kitchen. The blood on the floor said that Mullin had gone down into the staterooms.

"Mullin!" I shouted. "Come out!"

I didn't get a response and didn't imagine he was going to comply. I was merely trying to get an audible location.

"Mullin!" I shouted again.

Still, I heard nothing. I got off to the side and moved closer to the stairs that led down. I kept my back to the wall beside the stairwell. My pistol was up and ready. "Come on, Mullin. Let's end this and get you and Frank some help," I said. "He's going to bleed out if he doesn't get medical attention soon." I hoped the mention of his brother would get a reaction. The truth was, Frank was more than likely already dead, and I didn't care too much about Mullin's wellbeing. I heard a rustling from below and then what sounded like a groan.

"Come on up," I said. "The Coast Guard is on the way."

With my back to the wall beside the stairway, I got as low as possible and quickly poked out into the opening for a look down. The moment I did, I saw Mullin standing in the lower hallway with his aim on the stairs. I yanked my head back and dove away from the stairwell. Gunshots rang out—five or more, I didn't count. Bits of wood flew through the air. I landed belly down, quickly rolled over, and got my aim on the stairs. The wood wall I'd had my back to a moment earlier was splintered outward from the bullets. I kept my aim on the stairwell, but Mullin didn't come.

I got on my belly and crawled to the wall beside the stairwell. With my gun in my left hand, I aimed it around the corner and downward. I squeezed off three quick rounds and retreated backward. As I slid away, more return fire came. Again, wood splintered from the wall. A little too close for comfort. That time I counted his rounds—four shots. He could have very well had extra ammo stashed somewhere on the yacht. He could have had another weapon somewhere. He could have had an extra gun magazine. But if he didn't, he was almost out of bullets—which would make two of us.

The last round of return fire was a hell of a lot closer than the first. If I was going to try to get him to fire again, it had to be in a different direction. I quickly leapt across the opening of the stairwell while looking and aiming down. A full-size stainless steel refrigerator gave me cover on the far side. I didn't see Mullin in the hallway below, and no shots came when I'd crossed the room. I stayed pressed against the refrigerator door and swung my pistol into the stairwell. I fired off another three rounds and ducked closer to the dishwasher for cover. No return fire came. I quickly dropped my magazine from my gun and checked it—only four rounds left, and I didn't have another magazine, having given my spare to Tillerson earlier.

I waited. Thirty seconds passed. It could have been a minute. I had to wait until I clearly had him in my sights, but it didn't look like he was going to come to me. I inched nearer the stairwell when the window directly across from me exploded inward. Something slammed me in the chest and sent me back to the dishwasher.

Before I could react, I was hit again. Gunshots rang in my ears. My head and line of sight snapped up. Mullin stood outside a blown-out window with dead aim at me. I brought my gun up and fired my four shots. Mullin remained in the window. He aimed directly at my face.

I could see the slide on my gun locked back—I was empty. Mullin fired twice and disappeared backward from the window. I looked to my left. Two holes were in the dishwasher door, not more than an inch from where my head had to have been. I quickly got my feet beneath me, stood, and crossed the room through the shattered glass. Blood covered the exterior of the yacht around the window. Mullin's face-down body floated twenty feet away, his arms out to the sides, bobbing with the waves. I looked down to see a pair of round holes in the front of my suit jacket. I saw blood. My heart raced. I dropped my weapon to the floor and pulled my shirt down, ripping off four buttons to inspect the area. My vest had caught only one of the two shots.

CHAPTER 38

"It's fine," I said. "Go sit down."

My father gave me a look of disapproval, snatched the platter of bratwurst and steaks from my hand, and jammed a bottle of beer into my gut. "You just hold onto that."

I shook my head, took the beer, and plopped down in my chair. I twisted off the beer cap and pitched it on the table. My father walked the platter to the grill. The meat sizzled, and smoke rolled up into the air as he tossed everything on.

"What do you want?" my dad asked.

I looked over at him staring down at Lucky at his ankle—she'd been lying in a hole she'd dug in the yard, but apparently she'd come to give my father some puppy-dog eyes in hopes of getting some grill scraps.

"The little steak on the grill is hers. She likes hers rare. Make mine just a touch above that."

"You got it," he said. "What were your mom and Amy working on in there?"

"Salad, I think."

"Salad?" he scoffed. "Hopefully of the potato variety." He came to the table, pulled out a chair, and had a seat. "I thought I saw your mom making some kind of dessert or something before."

"Banana cream pie. And she made three of them," I said. "Because apparently two of them wasn't enough."

"You know how she is when she gets on the baking thing."

"Yeah," I said.

My dad jerked his chin at me. "How's the arm?" he asked. "Or armpit, I should say?"

The bullet that my vest didn't catch passed directly through a bit of pectoral meat and did a pretty good job of slicing through the flesh under my arm. The wound required some stitches and an "If this had been an inch to the left" talk from the doctor. The reality was that it was mostly a graze, and the sling the doctor gave me to wear was simply to limit my range of motion and the chances of popping a stitch. The sling was somewhere in the house, next to whatever pain medicine they prescribed that I never took out of the bag. A beer or two and a couple of aspirin was all that was necessary for pain, and I was smart enough to limit my arm movements to not cause further damage. "It's fine," I said. "Once everything is all healed up, I'm probably going to need to have the tattoos that go under my arm touched up."

"You and those fancy tattoos," he said.

"You said they were stupid when I was younger."

"The ones you had when you were younger were stupid," he said.

"Fair enough."

"And the head?" he asked. "How's that?"

"Same," I said. "I'm good, Dad." It was the third time that day he'd asked me how everything was—my mother was up to somewhere around five or six times. Amy had asked only twice. I started to think I should get a sign to hang around my neck that said I was okay.

I lifted my hand and rubbed my fingertips over the twenty-some stitches from where I got pistol-whipped. The doc said I'd had a concussion, and having had one in the past, it netted me a week off work, or paid leave until I could pass some concussion test that I was scheduled for, and planned on passing, the upcoming week. I grabbed my beer and took a sip.

"Glad you're all right," he said. "We were pretty worried when we got the call that you were shot and at the hospital." He stood from his chair and checked on the grill.

"The call came from me," I said.

He grabbed the tongs and turned toward me. "I know. I was just saying that we were worried."

"Well, obviously it couldn't have been too bad if I was the one calling."

My father shrugged and turned the meat on the grill. "So, did they find anything else out about these two brothers?"

"Not much more than we already knew. The one who was working undercover decided he liked the criminal lifestyle and started his own little enterprise. Guess he brought his brother in on it. Hell, I shouldn't say 'little' enterprise. Almost fifty million in cash was recovered between the vans at the house and the yacht."

"What about all the killing?" he asked.

I took another pull from my beer. "Why or how it all went south and why everyone got killed, we don't really know. The thinking at the station was that these two got wind that the police were sniffing around and were trying to close up shop, so to speak, and flee the country. The DEA swooped in and took over everything on the case, so we'll only get what they want to give us moving forward. All we really know for certain is that all the deaths inside the carpet-cleaning businesses were attributed to Frank Mullin. A pair of guns recovered from a van at the house had his prints on them. I guess someone matched the guns to the retrieved rounds from the bodies."

The sound of a car's rumbling exhaust took over the Thursday evening tranquility. The car revved twice, and the exhaust note popped, gurgled, and cracked.

"What the hell is that?" my dad asked.

"I'm going to guess Steve in the driveway. He said he picked up his new car and was going to head over with it after work." I got the time from my watch—a couple of minutes after six. "And it's about after-work time." I scooped up my beer and rose from my chair. "Let me go investigate."

"If it is him, tell him to stop acting like a jackass."

I chuckled and walked from the backyard and past my boat on the side of the house. Past the Bronco, I could see the front of a bright red car. With another few steps, I saw Steve standing outside the driver's door.

Steve swung the door closed. "How are you—"

I cut him off, "I'm fine before you ask."

"Good," he said. Steve wore a goofy grin like a kid in a

candy store. "Well? What do you think?"

The car was a new Camaro, a ZL1 1LE. I knew that because Steve hadn't shut up about the thing for the last few weeks. I knew every spec the car had and how it was basically a race car with a radio. Steve had gone on and on about the cars it could "destroy" on a track. It was a sharp-looking car but completely useless for a day-to-day automobile. Not that my Bronco was going to win any awards in that category.

"Looks like it's begging for a speeding ticket," I said.

"Ack." He balked and waved away my comment.

"Are you happy with it?"

"Hell yeah. The GN was quick, but this thing is on another level. As soon as it's broken in, I'm going to hit some track days with her. See what she can really do."

"Sure," I said. "I was thinking about doing the same with the Bronco."

"The race you're looking for with your truck is called a Demolition Derby," Steve said.

I laughed.

"Do you want to drive it?" Steve asked.

I looked over the flat black hood with half of the motor protruding. The rest of the cherry-red car shined in the sun. It was flawless. "Nah, the last time I drove one of your cars, I totaled it," I said. "Probably best if I don't drive this one until it's got a few miles on it."

"Good point. Hop in. I'll spin you around the block quick."

"We were just about to eat," I said.

"Just get in. I'll have you back in five," he said.

"All right. All right. Don't piss off my neighbors," I said. "Or get us pulled over."

"I'm not gonna get us pulled over." Steve laughed. "I can't really open her up until about fifteen hundred miles. Break-in period and all."

I squeezed into the suede passenger seat and closed the door. Steve got behind the wheel and spent a minute or two talking about different driving modes before he pulled out of the driveway in Track mode.

Each bump in the road was jarring. The exhaust was only a fraction less loud inside the car than out. Steve pulled from my subdivision and gave the car some gas. The tires, which Steve had said were basically slicks, broke free. He sawed at the wheel and laughed. The car's power was ridiculous.

"Anything new at work?" I asked.

"Nothing since the woman in her garage and the man and woman in the condo that Tavaras owned. Aside from them, we've been quiet on anything new. Dave too. Making up for all the bullshit with Mullin, I guess."

"Hear anything on that?"

Steve checked his blind spot and switched lanes.

"We found out that Frank Mullin had once worked security at the old horse track. Guessing that's how he knew of the place. Aside from that, not much that you don't already know. I imagine what we know is probably the extent of what we'll find out too. The DEA isn't going to tell us anything. Halloway made a couple calls to the local bureau. They aren't talking about Mullin. Won't say a word about him. They claim that they're running an internal investigation or some garbage like that, and that's the end of it."

"Basically, they don't want to talk about something that they had brewing under their nose and were unaware of."

"Basically," Steve said. He downshifted the car for the upcoming red light. The exhaust cracked and burbled as we coasted to a stop. "Catch any of the press coverage?"

"A little," I said. "Seems it's good for ratings to have a rogue cop or fed or whatever you want to call Mullin starting a drug empire and racking up a body count in the twenties."

"Yeah. It would seem so," Steve said. "So, what's on the menu at the house? Smelled like you had the grill going."

"Steak, brats, some salad, and sides. Mom made banana cream pies."

"Hmm," he said.

"You want to stay for dinner?" I asked.

"I think Sasha's waiting on me. Plus, you've got the parents here."

"Call her and tell her to shoot over," I said. "We've got plenty of food to go around."

"Yeah, maybe," Steve said. "What the hell is with this stoplight?"

"It's a long one," I said.

"You know what. Here, let me try this."

"Try what?" I asked.

"Launch control," he said. "You're not really supposed to use it until the car is broken in, but this is, like, the perfect street."

"How is this the perfect street?"

"Flat. Straight. Nicely paved. No cars." He pressed a couple of buttons and brought the RPMs up.

The traffic light flashed green, and we shot forward. My head pressed back into the seat. Steve ripped the shifter into second gear then jammed it forward into third. The car roared. He let off the gas, and the exhaust popped and barked.

"This thing pulls like a mule," he said.

"Yeah," I said. "It's fast." A faint sound grew over the rumble of the car. I recognized the sound a split second later as I leaned forward and got a look at the passenger door mirror. A smile grew across my face.

I saw Steve's eyes rise to his rearview mirror.

"Aw, son of a…" he said. His head snapped toward me. "Don't even say it."

The End

For more books by E.H. Reinhard, please visit:
http://ehreinhard.com/

Made in the USA
Monee, IL
12 June 2024